Sunshine State EMP Blackout

Showdown

Blood is Thicker Series: Book two

St. Augustine •

I0677990

Punta Gorda •

Miami•

BRUNO BRENNAN

Sunshine State EMP Blackout

Showdown

Blood is Thicker Series: Book two

St. Augustine ●

Punta Gorda ●

Miami ●

BRUNO BRENNAN

SIGN UP FOR MY NEWSLETTER

Be the first to know about new book releases, see behind the scenes content and more.

BrunoBrennan.com

For my family, who despite each of our differnces or disagreements, I know we will always be there for one another because
"Blood is Thicker than Water"

Be sure to check out the first book in the
Blood is Thicker Series
Sunshine State EMP Blackout
"Family Reunion"

Available in Paperback, Ebook and Audiobook

INTRODUCTION

Maria had been through hell and back, but she was strong, stronger than anyone could imagine. But now, she had to confront her past, face the man who had caused all that pain. Chuck Warner, the man she had once loved, the man she had thought would be the love of her life. But he had turned out to be a monster, a ruthless killer, a man who cared for nothing but power and control. He had to be stopped and maybe she was the only person that could appeal to whatever humanity he had left, if any. She had to try, even if it meant losing the new love she had found with Joe. She hoped to return to his arms, but there were no guarantees.

After discovering Maria had slipped away in the night, Joe felt a deep sense of loss, devastation, fear and anger wash over him. He knew he couldn't stop her, that she had to do this on her own. But the thought of her facing that monster alone terrified him. He had to find a way to protect her, to be there for her when she needed him the most. He had to get Maria back or die trying.

Joe turned to his companions, the group of survivors who had become his family. They shared a look of determination, a resolve to stand by each other no matter what lay ahead. They would face the dangers that lurked in the shadows, the uncertainties that threatened to tear them apart. They would fight for their survival, for their freedom, for their future.

Joe Kelly knew one thing for sure, he had to have Maria in his life. Now that love had once again entered his heart, he could never live without her. With the support of his family they would deal with the evils of Chuck Warner and bring Maria home again where she would be safe, and they could finally begin building a future and find some peace in this chaotic world.

TABLE OF CONTENTS

CHAPTER ONE:
THE RELUCTANT FAREWELL

After all they had gone through to finally reach the relative safety of the cabin, Joe was in disbelief that Maria could just up and leave all on her own to face down a madman. He understood her motives trying to reason with a man she had once loved enough to marry. Maybe seeing her, might shame Chuck Warner into change, but he doubted it. Power had a strong intoxicating allure to many men and once they had it, it was a hard thing to let go of.

Joe clung to the letter Maria had left him before sneaking away in the night.

"My dearest Joe,

By the time you read this, I will be gone. I am so sorry for leaving without discussing it with you first. I know you will be angry with me and deeply hurt, but please try to understand - confronting Chuck is something I must do alone.

I can't begin to express my sorrow and shame

over the atrocities Chuck has committed. To think the man, I once loved could be responsible for such evil horrifies me. Everything I knew has been turned upside down.

In the short time we've known each other, I've come to care for you more deeply than I ever thought possible, especially after the heartbreak of my failed marriage. You showed me that true love still exists in this world. Every moment we've shared has been precious to me. I will always carry the memories of our time together in my heart.

Which is why I need you to know that leaving was agonizing. But finding out the man responsible for so much suffering is my own husband...I can't ignore that. There is too much history and too many unresolved feelings. I have to face Chuck myself and appeal to any shred of goodness left in him. I know him better than anyone. Perhaps I am the only one who stands a chance of reaching what's left of his humanity.

I realize it's dangerous and you'll be angry with me. But this is my burden to bear. All I can do is pray that we'll be reunited when it's over. My only wish is to help end this nightmare, then return to your arms where I belong.

No matter how this ends, please remember one

thing - you gave me hope again when I had lost everything. My heart is forever yours. I love you, Joseph Kelly. Wait for me.

Yours always,

Maria"

Reading it over and over through his tears. His heart, now broken, but filled with resolve to get her back in his arms once again.

Joe gathered around the dying embers of the campfire alongside Jojo, Jake, Claire, and Sam. A warm welcome from the cool morning chill. Joe wasted no time filling them in on the past relationship between Maria and Chuck. As soon as he shared Maria's letter, the group exchanged horrified looks.

"Joe, you can't be serious," Jake said. "This Chuck fella sounds dangerous as hell. If Maria turns up there alone, he'll eat her alive."

"All the more reason we need to move fast," Joe growled. He quickly summarized the depraved acts Chuck had already committed in Leesburg. Jaws clenched around the fire as the reality of Maria's peril sank in.

"I ain't losing her now that we've found each other, I can't," Joe said gruffly, his gravelly voice tinged with desperation. "But I can't do this without you all."

He looked at each of them beseechingly. "She's family now. And we protect our own, no matter what it takes. Are you with me or not?"

Jojo stood immediately, clapping a hand on his father's shoulder. "I'm with you, Pops. To hell and back."

One by one, Jake, Sam, and Claire also voiced their support. Joe's lined face softened with gratitude. These men and women had become his brothers in arms over their long journey here together. Now they would walk through fire to save one of their own.

"So, what's this bastard look like so I can put a bullet 'tween his eyes?" Sam asked in his usual laconic drawl, idly spinning a bowie knife in his calloused hands.

A ghost of a smile touched Joe's mouth. Sam's casual ferocity never failed to reassure him. But Chuck's villainy ran deeper than any one man.

"Won't be that simple, I'm afraid," Joe sighed. "His whole damn troop of degenerates needs putting down before this is over. But one step at a time."

He turned to Jake who had been studying a map by firelight, brow furrowed in concentration. "You figure the best way into that hellhole yet?"

Jake traced his finger along the winding backroads. "I reckon we can slip in under the cover of darkness if we keep off the main highway and stick to the tree lines. Won't be easy though. May have to go in on foot the last few miles. I'll scout ahead when we get close, see what we're up against."

Joe nodded, satisfied. Though young, Jake's competency in navigating and tracking equaled any man's.

"Grab everything we've got that's useful for combat and medical," Joe said. "Then load up the van. We'll move out once we've gotten geared up. I'd like to get as close as we can before hiding the van in the woods. Then as Jake said, we'll go in on foot from there. We can set up some sort of a basecamp that we make our observations from. We'll probably have to make some scouting runs from there to try and find any weaknesses we might be able to exploit."

The group dispersed to gather supplies with militaristic efficiency. Having planned for this day, Joe's underground bunker was well-stocked with weapons and ammo. He tossed guns, knives, bulletproof vests and gear into duffel bags while Jojo gathered medical supplies, flashlights, and tools.

Within thirty minutes their battered old van was

packed to the brim. Joe did a last weapons check then slammed the rear doors with an air of grim finality. As he turned to take one last look at the cabin that had become their sanctuary, Joe sent up a silent prayer they would all return from this alive.

Stowing his gear in the passenger seat, Joe slid behind the wheel just as the first faint glow appeared along the eastern horizon. The others climbed into the van, weariness etched on their faces but determination in their eyes.

Jake broke the uneasy silence as they bumped down the rutted gravel driveway. "We'll get her back, Joe. Just gotta stay smart and watch each other's six, like old times."

Though he nodded, Joe's stomach was in knots, the miles between him and Maria feeling insurmountable. Gripping the wheel until his knuckles turned white, he focused only on the way ahead.

As the cabin disappeared behind them in the rearview mirror, Joe's jaw tensed. He would move heaven and earth to bring Maria home or die in the attempt. She was a part of him now in a way he'd never thought possible again late in life. The chance to love once more was worth fighting for.

"Hang on sweetie, I'm coming for you," Joe whispered

into the cool morning wind rushing by outside. Then he pushed the gas pedal down harder, propelling them forward into the perilous unknown.

* * * * * * * * * * * * * * * * * * * *

The van ate up miles of cracked asphalt bathed in predawn light. Jojo leaned forward, bracing one hand against the back of Jake's seat. The other hovered near the hunting knife sheathed on his belt. Though his mind was weary, years of combat training had honed Jojo's senses to a razor's edge. One hand on his blade, he continuously scanned their surroundings, alert for threats.

In the very back, Claire and Sam sorted medical supplies, taking stock of their meager first aid options. By necessity Claire had become the group's de facto medic. Though the pressure of such responsibility weighed on her, she focused solely on preparing for the mission ahead. Lives would depend on her skills and nerves of steel.

Sam worked with silent, methodical focus alongside Claire. His stoicism hid a wisdom beyond his years. In battle he was as steady as stone, acting with decisive grace. Now he reviewed tactical plans in his mind, running through every variable and outcome.

The miles unfurled ahead as the tension inside

the van thickened. Each bump in the road rattled their nerves raw. But they remained resolute. For Joe's sake they would brave the bowels of hell itself to bring Maria home.

As the first crude structures of Leesburg's outskirts took shape in the distance, Jake scanned the terrain anxiously through a pair of worn binoculars. His youthful features creased into a frown.

"Not liking what I'm seeing here folks," Jake said. "Main road's pretty well guarded already. We try coming straight in, they'll light us up like the Fourth of July."

"Shit," Joe spat. The relatively clear highway ahead seemed their quickest route into the viper's nest to find Maria. But Jake was right - a direct assault would be suicide. Joe slammed a palm against the steering wheel in frustration. They needed another way.

"Hold up now, don't go losing your head," Sam drawled calmly from the back. "We knew this wasn't gonna be a cakewalk. I'd wager there's back ways in if we're clever about it. Right, Jake?"

Jake gave a terse nod, intently studying the map again. A glimmer of hope flickered in Joe's chest. If anyone could find them a path through, it was Jake.

For several tense minutes the only sounds were the rumbling engine and the rustling of Jake's map.

Then finally he looked up, a light in his eyes.

"I got it. There's an old utility road, looks like it runs parallel to Main Street but a good half mile or so off far as I can tell. We'd have to go in on foot through the woods. But I think it's our best shot at slipping by unnoticed."

Joe considered Jake's proposed route, idly stroking his beard. Traveling by foot at night through unknown woods was risky. But if it got them to Maria, he was willing to pay the price.

"Alright, let's give this utility road a try once we're a few miles out," Joe said at last. "Nice work finding us a side door, son."

Pride swelled in Jake's chest at the praise from his taciturn father-in-law. Maybe he had gained a few valuable skills on this harrowing journey after all. Jake could feel his relationship with Joe growing stronger since they had arrived at the cabin and he loved it.

As the decrepit outskirts of Leesburg took shape around them, Joe pulled the van beneath the cover of the woods that lined each side of the road to wait for full darkness. As the group exited the van, Jojo stretched his aching muscles. Joe looked around. "Alright everyone, we've still got quite a few hours until it gets dark enough to move out, so let's take this time to get our gear ready. I don't want to make a camp here, I think we need to make some sort of base camp closer to town. Let's grab everything we can reasonably carry and if we need more later, we'll just have to come back here. Also let's do our best to get the van camouflaged as best as we can before we leave."

While Joe took a final walk-around, Jojo dug through their disguises and supplies for anything useful. He handed a bag to each person. "Here, try to blend in with these if we encounter anyone once we're inside. I grabbed whatever might help us look less conspicuous."

Claire peeked inside her bag curiously. It contained a tattered scarf, fingerless gloves, and other garments that had seen better days. Though worn, the clothing would help them avoid standing out on the streets of Leesburg.

"Good thinking," Claire said. "These could make the difference if we come across trouble." Jojo flushed at the praise. Impressing level-headed Claire, even with this small act, buoyed his confidence.

As the final rays of sunlight disappeared, Joe signaled it was time to move out. On foot they struck out through the dense tree line, avoiding the main road now slick with shadows. They could only hope the utility path ahead lived up to Jake's estimation.

Navigating by moonlight, they slipped through

the woods like ghosts, senses heightened. The hum of insects and their muffled footfalls were the only sounds. After nearly an hour, the narrow maintenance road Jake had pinpointed on the map finally emerged from the underbrush.

Halting, the group took cover in the tree line and studied the cracked asphalt strip beyond. It appeared disused but more importantly, deserted. Joe met Jake's eyes and nodded. The kid had delivered as promised. Their infiltration route was secured.

Moving silently in single file, they stuck to the road's crumbling edges, alert for any sign of activity in the dilapidated buildings ahead. The air seemed to crackle with tension. As the first structure took shape, the facade of a once-vibrant town now barely concealed the decay rotting it from within. Somewhere in its diseased heart, Maria waited. And Joe would lay waste to all of it to save her.

The moon dipped below the roofline of a listing warehouse, casting the road into deeper shadow. Jake froze, holding up a closed fist. Huddled forms lay just ahead, partially obscured by an overturned dumpster. Homeless citizens or Chuck's guards lying in ambush? There was only one way to know.

Carefully, Jake crept forward until the forms took shape in the darkness - a woman wrapped in threadbare blankets shielding two small children. As Jake backed away quietly so as not to disturb them, relief washed over the group. Sleeping innocents, not Chuck's thugs.

They continued on through the deathly silence hanging over the empty streets. The deeper they moved into Leesburg's wounded heart, the thicker the tension grew. Maria was here somewhere amid the decay. And Joe would tear it all down to bring her home.

CHAPTER TWO
MARIA'S CONFRONTATION

The sun beat down relentlessly as Maria approached the outskirts of New Leesburg on foot.

Swiping sweat from her brow, Maria steeled her nerves as the crude barrier surrounding the town came into view. She had no idea what awaited inside. The only thing propelling her forward was a naive hope that her husband Chuck still retained some shred of goodness that she could appeal to.

Two armed men stood guard at the barricaded entrance, assault rifles held casually across their chests. Their eyes roamed over Maria's petite frame lecherously as she drew nearer. One elbowed the other with a lewd grin. Maria's stomach turned but she kept her expression neutral.

"That's far enough, sweetheart," the first guard said as Maria halted before them. His wandering gaze lingered a beat too long on her cleavage. "What's your business here?"

Maria took a bracing breath. "I've come to see my husband, Chuck Warner. Please tell him I'm here."

The second guard guffawed. "Your husband? You expect us to believe a fine piece of ass like you is hitched to the mayor?"

The other man joined in the laughter. "She's probably looking to trade a little sugar for a hot meal. Ain't that right, darlin'?" He reached to chuck her under the chin mockingly.

Anger flared in Maria's chest. In one swift motion, she swatted the man's hand away and dealt a stinging open hand slap across his face.

"Don't touch me, you pig!" she spat. "I am Maria Warner, Chuck's wife. Now take me to him at once before I have your hides tanned!"

Shock registered on the men's faces as they processed her words. The guard Maria had slapped gingerly touched his reddening cheek, clearly embarrassed by her dressing him down. His partner seemed unsure whether to apprehend or obey her.

After a beat, the flustered guard finally radioed their superior for guidance. "Yeah, Sarge, we got a situation here. This lady claims to be the mayor's old lady..."

He relayed the details of their confrontation while Maria silently fumed. Just then, the walkie crackled to life with brusque orders - the mayor's wife was to be granted entry immediately and escorted to him right away.

With surly reluctance, the guards ushered Maria through the barricade at gunpoint. She held her head high, refusing to show fear. But internally, her heart hammered as she was marched through the dingy streets toward an uncertain reunion.

The once-vibrant town had decayed into squalor and neglect. Windows were broken, buildings defaced with graffiti. Hard-eyed citizens watched the passing guards warily before disappearing indoors like specters. Maria suppressed a shudder. What had become of her hometown?

At last, they arrived before an impressive brick structure - the former city hall. More armed men stood stationed outside. One looked Maria over dismissively before radioing inside.

After a brief exchange, he waved the group onward. Maria's mouth went dry, but she kept her bearing composed. She tried to ignore the weapons aimed squarely at her back ushering her inside.

The expansive lobby was in shambles, trash

and filth littering the cracked marble floors. They marched her down a gloomy corridor to an ornate set of oak doors. Her escorts knocked twice before entering.

"The mayor's wife, sir," the guard announced brusquely.

Maria's pulse roared in her ears. She could just make out Chuck's familiar silhouette behind a massive desk in the shadows. At the guard's declaration, he jerked ramrod straight in his high-backed leather chair.

"That'll be all. Leave us," Chuck ordered in his smoothly commanding voice. The guards retreated, closing the doors firmly behind them.

* * * * * * * * * * * * * * * * * * * *

Alone now, Maria's courage nearly failed her. She wanted nothing more than to flee this office and the monster masquerading as her husband within it. But she forced leaden feet forward instead.

Chuck looked much the same - handsome and imposing. But as Maria drew closer, the predatory glint in his sapphire eyes sent a chill down her spine. This was not the man she had once loved.

"Maria...you came back," Chuck said, clearly

shaken. He rose slowly, hands braced on the desk as if for balance.

Maria halted a careful distance away, face placid but heart racing. "I had to see you, to understand what's happened here." She nodded meaningfully around the dilapidated office.

Chuck straightened, regaining some of his composure. "Desperate times called for difficult decisions, that's all," he replied evasively. "But never mind that now. What matters is you're home, where you belong."

He stepped toward Maria with arms extended as if to embrace her. She recoiled sharply. Chuck withdrew, looking wounded by her rejection.

"Don't pretend you actually missed me, Chuck," Maria said coldly. "I know exactly the kind of depraved monster you've become since I left."

Chuck's eyes hardened into flinty chips. "Is that what you think of me?" he asked quietly. Maria could sense the gathering storm behind his controlled tone.

Refusing to be cowed, Maria unleashed the disgust and fury she had bottled up since learning of his vile deeds. She spat every gut-wrenching detail Joe had shared, watching Chuck's handsome face slowly contort in rage.

When Maria finally fell silent, cheeks flushed and chest heaving from her tirade, Chuck exploded.

"How dare you judge me!" he thundered. "You, who abandoned our home to selfishly forge a new life! You were content to leave me alone to salvage some kind of order amidst utter chaos and destruction. I did what was necessary to save these people!"

His spittle flew as he ranted, veins bulging in his neck. Maria stood frozen. This maniacal stranger both terrified and revolted her in equal measure. She had never seen Chuck's charming facade crack so completely.

"There's no justification for what you've done," Maria replied evenly once Chuck paused for breath. "You've become the very evil you claim to fight. Can't you see that?"

At her words, Chuck's expression warped into a mask of ugly rage. He crossed the space between them in two large strides and wrenched Maria's wrist viciously, causing her to cry out.

"You dare judge me?" he spat, face inches from her own. "You lost that right when you abandoned me!"

Maria wrenched her arm free, recoiling from him. Any naive hope of appealing to Chuck's conscience shriveled away. She now saw the depth of his corruption - his soul was as twisted as his actions. Her husband was beyond redemption.

But Maria was not beyond courage. With panic racing through her veins, she forced herself to soften her voice. If she had any hope of stopping Chuck from within, she needed him to believe her sympathies had changed.

"You're right, I made mistakes," Maria said, massaging her bruising wrist. "I was a fool not to stand by my man when things got difficult. But I want to make amends now."

Chuck's grip relaxed slightly but his eyes remained wary, searching Maria's face. She swallowed hard and continued her ruse.

"If you'll let me, I'd like us to start fresh, to build something good together from the ashes. I see now that you only want what's best for our people." Maria laid a timid hand on Chuck's chest beseechingly. "I'm here to help you however I can, my husband."

Chuck stared down at Maria, his rage shifting to something more calculating. Could he dare hope she had finally recognized all he had accomplished and wanted to share in his vision? The allure of having his queen ruling beside him once more held certain appeal.

"You can't imagine how long I've waited to hear such words from you," Chuck said thickly. He lightly clasped her hand against his chest. "I knew you'd come around eventually."

Maria forced herself not to pull away from his touch, every nerve screaming in revulsion. She allowed none of that to show on her face.

"I just need some time to process everything," Maria said, playing the part of blushing bride. "Give me a chance to walk the town, see how you've made life better here. To remember why I fell in love with you from the start."

Chuck considered this, his eyes roving hungrily over Maria. At last he nodded. "Very well. I'll have quarters prepared for your stay. Take all the time you need to...acclimate."

Maria exhaled in relief. She had bought herself a reprieve, if only temporarily. Time enough to assess Chuck's hold on the town and hopefully find a way to undermine him.

Chuck escorted her to the foyer, snapping his fingers to summon guards to show Maria to her room. But as she turned to leave, he caught her wrist once more, firmly this time. His breath was hot on her ear as he leaned in close.

"Don't toy with me, Maria," Chuck warned softly. "I'll be keeping a close eye on you during this little reconnaissance of yours. For both our sakes, I hope your change of heart is genuine, and I'll be sure to visit you in your room. It's been quite a while since I've been able to enjoy my bride."

With that ominous threat, he released her. Maria shot him a coy smile as she massaged her wrist, determined not to show weakness. "I would expect nothing less, my dear."

With her head high, she spun on her heel and followed the guards upstairs, leaving Chuck to brood in the foyer below. But as soon as Maria was alone in the dingy little room, the brave facade crumbled. She collapsed onto the cot, sobbing wretchedly into a dirty musty pillow.

Despair and bone-deep revulsion gripped Maria as the reality of her situation sank in. The madman she had once loved held her trapped here now, his perverted whims her only protection from the same atrocities inflicted on so many.

She longed for the safety of Joe's arms with an ache that made her soul howl. But the warm refuge she had found fleetingly with him seemed a lifetime away now. Maria was utterly alone in her mission to stop the beast Chuck had become.

As her sobs gradually faded to ragged breathing, cold resolve hardened within Maria's chest. She had allowed herself this one moment of weakness. Now it was time to be strong, to face the monster on his own territory. If she failed, her best hope would be a quick death.

Maria straightened with that grim thought, dashing away any lingering tears. She refused to cower in this dingy room awaiting rescue or disaster. She would walk this fetid town with her head held high, hiding revulsion beneath a mask of wifely duty. And she would silently gather every detail needed to unravel Chuck's regime.

* * * * * * * * * * * * * * * * * *

Maria emerged the next morning wearing an embroidered dress found in the wardrobe, as if preparing to join Chuck for an elegant ball rather than surveying a decaying town. It bolstered her courage, this small act of defiance.

At the foot of the stairs, the guard assigned discretely to her wheeled around in surprise at her bold attire. Maria breezed past him as though he were invisible. "I want to get better acquainted with our fair city. Please escort me on a tour."

With no choice but to obey the mayor's wife, the guard trailed Maria resentfully as she glided down broken sidewalks in impractical heels. Her piercing gaze took in everything while she chatted airily about the lovely weather and charming architecture.

They passed alleys full of rag-clad urchins fighting viciously over scraps. Trash fires smoldered inside dented barrels. The cloying stench of death and bodily waste hung on the stale breeze. But Maria clung fiercely to her composure. She would not be cowed by the horrors Chuck had wrought.

Occasionally citizens emerged from dilapidated buildings to stand mute, observing Maria's passage. Their eyes reminded her of those she had seen in the internment camps in Bosnia during her years as a Red Cross nurse - haunted, desolate, stripped of light and hope. Each one cut Maria to the marrow. But she did not dare stop or speak to them under the watchful eye of her escort.

Near what had once been the bustling town square, Maria noted crude platforms erected at regular intervals, surrounded by armed guards. Townsfolk were ushered up the steps reluctantly to receive meager dolings of food or rationed medications. The whole operation had the mechanistic efficiency of a slave camp.

Rancid scents wafted on the breeze from somewhere nearby. Maria's escort deliberately quickened his pace, steering her away from the source. But she managed a brief glimpse down one squalid alley of emaciated bodies piled haphazardly atop each other like so much cordwood. A mass grave, Maria realized with horror.

Her fists clenched as she continued on through this twisted mockery of the town she once had called home. Everywhere she turned, more evidence of Chuck's merciless regime battered her spirit. She had no clue how to even begin dismantling the intricate web of fear and control he had spun. But she knew in her soul she must find a way.

Nearing the crumbling remains of the town hall, Maria begged a rest. Perching daintily on a concrete bench near a bed of wilted roses, she set her mind to analyzing all she had observed. The guard kept his distance, smoking sullenly while keeping one eye fixed on her at all times.

Certain truths became evident during Maria's reflection. Chuck's empire was a constantly shape-shifting creature with himself at the head and heart. Cutting off either would be the surest way to kill the beast. Without Chuck's cult of personality to hold sway, his web would crumble. But how to break that thrall?

As Maria pondered, a small boy wandered up and placed a scraggly dandelion at her feet. His mournful gray eyes peered up at her beseechingly before he scampered away like a frightened animal.

Moved to tears, Maria knew in that moment what she must do. These people needed reminding of their own humanity. And she must be the one to awaken it before Chuck's cruelty snuffed out their spirits entirely. Her course was clear, even if it invited death. She would ignite the flame of resistance and help give Chuck's victims the tools to dismantle his empire themselves.

Steeling her nerve, Maria rose and dusted off her dress. With a gracious nod to her escort, she turned back toward the town hall. She had seen enough for today. Now it was time to begin planning Chuck's downfall in earnest. However slim her chances, Maria was more determined than ever to bring his reign of terror crashing down or die in the attempt. This she solemnly vowed as she climbed the crumbling marble steps back into the viper's nest, head held high.

CHAPTER THREE
UNWELCOMED ARRIVAL

Joe's ex, Paulette had gone through hell to get to the cabin. She doubted she could have made it if she hadn't found Alicia along the way. Once strangers, they were now close traveling companions. Alicia having lost her father after the blackout and being abandoned by her mother years before, leaving her family behind for another man, mimicking Paulette's past behavior with her own family seemed to draw them closer together creating an unbreakable bond as they both were able to learn more about each other's past on this grueling trip. Paulette was still anguished over being sexually assaulted along the way, but grateful she was able to end that man's life before he had a chance to do the same to Alicia. She may not have been there much for her own daughter Taylor, but at least she was able to protect young Alicia.

Now as they walked, the trees opened up and they stepped into a clearing. Just ahead, nestled against the tree line, was the cabin. Paulette stopped short for a moment, staring at the grand structure that represented a past life with Joe she had long ago abandoned. Tears began to form as the memories of her past life with Joe and the kids came flooding back with a vengeance. Alicia gave her an encouraging look.

"No matter what happens, I'll be right here with you," she said kindly. Bolstered by her support, Paulette took a deep breath and continued forward. This was it - time to face the past she had tried so hard to forget.

As they walked closer step by step, Paulette could feel her nervousness rising, but she told herself to be strong and continue. She noticed strangers sitting out in front of the cabin around the campfire and approached slowly with caution.

The group turned to face them as Paulette called out nervously, "He- Hello there. Is Joe here?"

One of the ladies in the group responded, "No he and some of the others went into town, we don't know when they'll be back. Can we help you?"

Paulette looked defeated, "How about his son Jojo or his daughter Taylor, are they around?"

"Jojo went with him, Taylor is here though, I'll go get her for you." as the lady went inside.

A few moments later Taylor appeared at the door with young Parker straddled around her hip.

Taylor looked up sharply, her expression clouding over when she spotted her mother. Parker, sensing the shift in mood, began to fuss.

There was an awkward silence as mother and daughter looked at one another. The gulf of years and hurt feelings yawned between them. Paulette gazed at Taylor with a heart full of remorse, wishing she could find the right words to begin bridging that divide.

"Taylor..." she began haltingly. "You've grown into such a beautiful young woman."

Taylor's eyes narrowed. "No thanks to you," she said bluntly.

Paulette winced. She deserved that.

"You're right," she acknowledged. "I haven't been the mother I should have been. But I'm here now, and I intend to make things right between us... if you'll let me."

Taylor studied her mother through suspicious eyes. But seeing the sincerity in Paulette's face, her expression gradually softened.

"We'll see," was all she said. But there had been

a slight relaxation around her mouth and eyes. Paulette felt a flicker of hope. It would take time to regain Taylor's trust, but this was a start.

Looking over at Alicia, Taylor asked, "Who's your friend?"

Paulette putting her arm around her companion said, "This is Alicia, we met on the road and have become friends, she had nowhere to go and no family so I thought she might be welcomed here. Even if I'm not"

Taylor looking at her mother gave a deep sigh, "Mother, quit being so dramatic, you're both welcome to stay. I couldn't turn two people out with a clear conscience, no matter what the past. Now dad on the other hand, he might throw you out on your ass, but I'm sure he'd let your friend stay. You can take that up with him when he gets back."

Paulette, looking somewhat relieved, asked, "Taylor, where is your father and Jojo for that matter?"

Taylor shifting Parker on her hip said, "Well mother, that's kind of a long story. Come on inside and I'll get you caught up as best as I can."

CHAPTER FOUR
INTO THE LION'S DEN

The night air was heavy with moisture as Joe's rescue party slipped undetected into the outskirts of New Leesburg. They had abandoned the van on a remote backroad, miles out and proceeded on foot using overgrown trails only Jake's sharper survival skills could detect. Now, a sense of tense purpose electrified the group as they neared enemy terrain. Maria awaited somewhere within the decaying town ahead, and Joe's gut churned thinking of her in that monster's claws.

Squinting in the darkness, Joe spotted the hulking outline of what looked to be an old textile warehouse. Part of the roof had caved in, but the thick brick walls appeared largely intact. It would suit their purposes well for a covert base of operations while they planned Maria's extraction.

"Here, this'll do," Joe rasped to the others,

gesturing at the abandoned structure. One by one they crept up to the gaping entrance, senses on hyper alert for any sign of activity within or nearby. But only oppressive silence greeted them.

Sam took point, rifle sweeping back and forth methodically as he cleared each room. Finding nothing but old machinery and rat droppings, he motioned the all-clear. Jojo secured the busted front door as best he could while Jake set up some fishing lines tied across all the openings in the building as a crude but effective early perimeter warning system.

Claire immediately began taking inventory of their weaponry and medical supplies. She had become their de facto medic and armorer as perhaps the most clear-headed in combat situations. Joe knew the gravity of their mission weighed on all of their young shoulders, but maybe none more than Claire's.

Yet her slender hands remained steady as she calmly checked and rechecked gear. Looking at Claire's focused expression in the dimness, Joe was reminded suddenly of Maria. Both petite women possessed a deep well of hidden strength. Joe only prayed Maria could hold on long enough for them to reach her.

Unable to stand still, Joe paced the crumbling

warehouse floor like a caged animal. His mind churned tirelessly with plans to smash through Chuck's defenses and extract Maria, each one more perilous than the last. But he knew a direct assault was suicide. If Maria was being guarded, they needed a window into the organization from the inside. Power in numbers was now their only advantage.

Jake and Sam took shifts circling the perimeter of Chuck's headquarters, a grand old city hall building occupying an entire block of what was once downtown. Jojo stood watch with Claire, rifle in hand, as Joe continued to wear a path in the dusty concrete floor. None dared speak and break the fragile silence as midnight approached.

When Jake returned from his perimeter sweep, he signaled Joe over quickly. "You gotta hear this," Jake whispered, pulling Joe into the corner. "I was doing a lap around the back of Chuck's place when I overheard two of his grunts grousing loudly about shit pay and rotten work conditions."

Joe's brows shot up with interest. "That right?"

"Sounded like a couple of real malcontents to me," Jake continued. "Got me thinking we could maybe exploit that, try to flip them against ol' Chuck."

"Turn his own men against him," Joe muttered approvingly. "Now there's a damn good strategy. We'll need eyes and ears on the inside if we want half a prayer of grabbing Maria back."

Nodding vigorously, Jake replied, "Just what I was thinking. Sam's got a gift for persuasion, I figured he could make first contact, feel them out about going double agent."

Joe clasped Jake's shoulder firmly. "Good work. Let's pitch this to the others." Raising his voice, Joe quickly outlined Jake's proposal to recruit some of Chuck's disgruntled foot soldiers to their side. Sam nodded along eagerly as Joe spoke, his cunning mind already spinning strategies.

"If we dangle the prospect of better pay and treatment under new leadership, seems to me some of those boys would jump at the chance to stab Chuck in the back," Sam remarked once Joe finished.

Under the cover of darkness, Sam and Jake headed out an hour later to make first contact with the potential turncoats. Dressed in ratty street clothes, they looked the part of resistance recruiters.

Joe watched them slip away, fresh hope warring with old anxiety in his gut. Everything hinged on winning Chuck's minions over to their side. Their chances were feeble otherwise. Sam's confident wink as he ducked out the door helped bolster Joe's spirit. The scrappy young man had saved their asses more than once already on this hellish journey. Joe was willing to trust his judgment once again.

Left alone again to ponder endless scenarios, Joe's thoughts kept circling back to Maria like a lodestone. Was she locked away in some dank cell, cold and afraid? He shook his head, jaw clenched. His fiery nurse would never show such weakness, even under threat of torture or death.

Still, the not knowing ate at Joe's guts like a knife. He desperately needed intel about the conditions of her imprisonment and routine of those around her. Anything that might reveal a way in.

Some two hours later, Sam and Jake returned wearing triumphant grins. They'd made contact with not just the two men Jake had overheard, but a third they found drowning his sorrows at a seedy soup kitchen after walking off the job in disgust. All three had seemed receptive when approached privately with the seductive offer of payments and power positions under Joe's supposed resistance group.

Sam rubbed his hands together eagerly as he explained, "Cracking open Chuck's operation from the inside is definitely doable if we play this right. I laid the groundwork for more meetings. Just gotta reel them in slowly and easily before bringing them into the fold fully."

Joe listened intently, weighing the possibilities and pitfalls. Turning Chuck's own soldiers against him could be their ace in the hole. But rushing could spook them and blow the whole thing up in their faces. They needed leverage before trying anything drastic.

"Feel this out carefully," Joe agreed. "The safest bet is focusing on any intel to start. Guard rotations, blueprints, where Maria might be held. We make a move without knowing the layout, we're as good as dead."

The three men continued strategizing into the early morning hours. When the need for rest finally overcame him, Joe wearily shrugged off his gear and settled onto the dusty floor near Claire. Her watchful eyes seemed to glow in the darkness, guarding over them all. Joe's lids closed heavily; all his furious mental energies depleted. Before sleep claimed him, one final thought rose hazily to the surface - for the first time since recovering Maria's letter, hope flickered again in Joe's chest. With luck and skill, they just might pull this off yet.

CHAPTER FIVE
PREDAWN DECISIONS

The setting sun streaked the cracked sidewalks of New Leesburg in bloody hues as Maria trudged back toward her quarters in Chuck's stronghold. Another day of playing the doting wife while subtly stirring dissent behind Chuck's back had drained what scant reserves of energy she still possessed. All Maria wanted now was to collapse into bed and find oblivion in a dreamless sleep.

That fleeting hope died the instant she opened the door and spotted the slinky black dress laid out conspicuously on the dingy sheets. Maria froze, a coil of dread twisting in her gut. Propped against the pillow was a note in Chuck's bold penmanship:

Dearest Wife,

I will expect you to wear this tonight when I pay you a visit after supper. We have lost too much time and I eagerly anticipate enjoying my husbandly rights once more now that you've returned. I trust you'll be appropriately attired and receptive to rekindling our passionate bond.

Eternally Yours,

Chuck

The paper crumpled in Maria's clenched fist. How dare he presume to summon her like some courtesan! She had half a mind to confront Chuck immediately and end this charade, consequences be damned. But suicide was not in Maria's nature. And so she swallowed the venom rising in her throat and set to mentally preparing for the violation ahead.

In the adjacent bathroom, Maria grimly stripped and stepped beneath the trickling shower, trying futilely to scrub away the shame and fury burning through her veins. What she wouldn't give for one of Joe's tender embraces now! But those days were gone, if they had ever existed outside stolen moments in her imagination. Her body and her wits were the only weapons left to wield against the monster Chuck had become. Maria intended to use both mercilessly as needed to destroy him or die trying.

After roughly toweling off, Maria stood before the cracked mirror studying her naked form. Ribs jutted through sallow flesh and her collarbones carved sharp ridges above sagging breasts. Not the tempting courtesan's body Chuck likely envisioned. Good, Maria thought bitterly. Let the sight of her repulse and disappoint him. She needn't make his depraved use of her too enticing.

Resigned to her gruesome task, Maria shimmied into the sleazy black dress. It clung lewdly to her gaunt curves like a macabre funeral shroud. Appropriate garb, she mused, for the impending death of her self-worth and Chuck's innocence she once cherished. Both must be sacrificed upon this altar to topple the high priest of New Leesburg.

Maria paced the close confines of her locked quarters like a caged panther as the sky darkened outside. Each passing minute wound her coil of dread tighter until she thought it might snap her spine. When distant chimes signaled the dinner hour, Maria's heart began thunderously outpacing the tolling bells. This was it - her corrupted Faustian bargain struck at last.

Right on cue, a key rattled in the lock and Chuck strode in, long coat swirling. His sapphire eyes raked over Maria in her whorish costume, full lips curling into a wolfish grin of approval.

"Exquisite," he purred. "Just what I envisioned.

Come greet your husband properly."

Maria's stomach heaved as Chuck embraced her forcefully, his hot breath steaming her neck as he nuzzled and fondled her with almost bestial urgency. She fought the primal urge to sink her teeth into his jugular and tear out his throat.

When Chuck's lips claimed hers ruthlessly, Maria struggled not to vomit down his front. Eyes closed; she willed her mind far away to tranquil lakesides with Joe while enduring Chuck's unwelcome plunder. He could degrade her flesh, but never conquer her spirit. She clung fiercely to that fact as Chuck shoved her toward the mussed bed.

The full weight of Chuck's body crushed the air from Maria's lungs as he pawed at her skimpy dress, baring her shrunken breasts. As Chuck's head dipped to her chest, Maria arched her back, digging her nails into his shoulders until they scraped bone, drawing blood. Let the bastard take his pleasure, but not without sharing her pain.

Chuck hardly seemed to notice Maria's violence, so lost was he in rapacious mania. He stood up towering over her as she lay on the bed. He started to slowly unbutton his pants, lower his zipper and finally dropped his pants to the floor. He motioned to Maria and she knew what she had to do for this vile man. Holding back tears and trying to keep a smile she took him into her mouth. It seemed like an eternity before he finally flipped her roughly onto all fours and drove into her savagely from behind. Dry agony lanced through Maria's core. She had made love to Chuck many times in the past as husband and wife, but this was nothing like those times. Silent tears carved hot trails down her hollowed cheeks as Chuck rutted into her relentlessly.

When Chuck finally spent himself with a satisfied groan, Maria collapsed forward onto the mattress, feeling his seed ooze down her thigh. A numb void hollowed her out. She was but a carved-out vessel for Chuck to fill and discard at will. He would never truly possess her soul where Joe still dwelled.

As they lay side by side in the oppressive darkness, Chuck idly stroked Maria's limp hair. "I'm so very pleased to have you back in my bed where you belong, my sweet," he murmured. "Tomorrow, we start making plans to expand our little empire. But first I'll need to purge a few rats. I'm sure you've heard the ugly rumors of rebellion brewing."

Maria's pulse quickened, though she kept her voice carefully disinterested while gently stroking Chuck's bare chest. "Just idle gossip I'm sure. You're too beloved for any real dissent."

Chuck's chest rumbled with sinister laughter. "If only that were true! No, the people's love is fickle, I've learned. Far better they fear me. Dissenters will face swift justice."

He described in chilling detail his plans for mass public executions to quell any rebels. Maria hung raptly on every word, burning them into memory to better take advantage of them at a later time.

Oblivious to Maria's true loyalties, Chuck prattled on about his ironclad security measures and unbreachable inner sanctum. Valuable intelligence if it could only reach the right ears. Maria continued playing the doting, dumbfounded wife, softly stroking his now limp manhood coaxing more secrets from Chuck's loose lips.

When he had finally talked himself out, Chuck rolled atop Maria again, this time quickly spilling his seed across her stomach before collapsing into snores beside her. Repulsed, Maria wiped away the viscous fluid with the soiled sheets. Sleep would elude her tonight. She remained rigidly awake plotting Chuck's demise, more determined than ever.

At first light, Maria rose quietly and reached for Chuck's discarded overcoat hanging nearby. She rifled carefully through its pockets until her fingers closed around a solid metal key and folded paper. Hands shaking, she unfurled the paper by the window's gray light, scanning its contents feverishly. A map of hidden tunnels beneath the town's streets - Chuck's secret escape route if his stronghold fell! This changed everything.

Maria studied the map until she had fixed it clearly in memory. Chuck mumbled in his sleep, making her blood run cold. Hurriedly she refolded the map precisely and slipped the key back into Chuck's coat lining. With these secrets, Chuck's inner sanctum could be breached or be used to elude capture if everything went to shit. Maria felt a new hope rising like dawn's light. Today marked a turning point; she was sure of it.

Chuck departed sometime before Maria awoke again. She listened at the door, confirming her regular guard had returned. Good, she preferred his silent contempt to Chuck's serpentine endearments. Dressing demurely, Maria emerged to resume her guise of a loyal wife walking among the people. Chuck's offhand remark about sedition needed to be urgently shared.

Maria went through the motions - praising Chuck's vision to guards in the square, lauding his "mercy" to the wretched beggars seeking her favor.

Inside, she burned with urgency to pass on Chuck's plans for violent suppression.

That evening, Maria employed her burgeoning skills in deception to pump Chuck for more information as he drank himself into a lustful stupor. With the right questions and feigned ignorance, she pried loose the identities of his most trusted inner circle who could expose his weaknesses. Sprawled snoring on the bed, Chuck had no clue of the power he had relinquished into Maria's hands this night. Let him rest while he still could. A reckoning was coming at long last to New Leesburg and Maria intended to be the vessel of Chuck's downfall or die in the attempt.

CHAPTER SIX
PLANTING SEEDS OF DOUBT AND HOPE

The rendezvous point was a crumbling mausoleum near the desolate town cemetery. Under the light of a pale half-moon, the two groups arrived from opposite directions, each man's head swiveling warily to scope new surroundings. These clandestine meetings nurtured suspicion as much as goodwill.

Joe hung back in the shadows as Jake and Sam took the lead on cultivating their budding alliance with the three disaffected guards. Keegan, Darryl and Boyd were their names according to Sam. Each had grown increasingly disenchanted working under Chuck's iron rule. Tonight, that discontent would either bind them together against a shared oppressor or doom them all.

As the men exchanged terse greetings, Joe studied their faces, searching for any hint of deception. But all he saw in their dirty, unshaven mugs was weariness and guarded optimism. These were desperate men seemingly trapped in untenable circumstances, ripe for flipping. Sam just needed to tap the right motivations and push the right buttons. No one could work a mark better.

"We took a huge risk meeting you again," Keegan muttered, his eyes darting around nervously. "If we're caught even whispering to rebel types, Chuck will mount our heads on spikes."

"And that's exactly why you need us," Sam replied smoothly. He eased in closer, keeping his voice low and earnest. "We're offering a way out, a chance at the good life you deserve. You really want to keep hauling Chuck's water until you inevitably end up on his hit list someday? We know you three have got useful skills and knowledge to share. All we ask is a little intel in return. Fair trade, far as I can tell."

The men shifted uncertainly at Sam's words. His talent for reading people told him they were hooked; they just needed a gentle push to be reeled in fully. He decided to offer up some irresistible bait.

"In fact, to show our good faith we come bearing gifts." Sam nodded to Jake who came forward holding three large sacks, clinking softly. The guards' eyes widened as they opened the bags to find food, smokes, ammo and a gun in each. They looked back and forth between the bags and Sam, hunger plain in their eyes. Sam crossed his arms casually over his broad chest. "Consider that a small taste to win your trust. You work with us, there's plenty more where that came from. Maybe even safe passage up north if this whole town goes tits up. We look after our own. Plus, if we are successful, you guys will be on the ground floor, you will be the ones who will get the leadership positions. You will be the ones that make the rules, no longer the grunts you currently are. No more doing as you're told, only to get the scraps the current leaders leave for you. So, what do you say?"

Darryl was the first to extend his hand to Sam. "I say you've got yourself a deal. We're in." The other two quickly followed suit as Sam beamed and grasped each of their hands warmly. More allies recruited to the good fight.

The men huddled close, speaking in hushed tones as they forged the beginnings of their clandestine partnership. Joe kept watch a few yards removed, close enough to signal Sam if anything seemed amiss. But the men seemed relaxed and open as they hashed out next steps.

Sam steered the conversation toward intel gathering, wanting to tap every resource they could. He asked pointed questions about guard rotations, weapon stockpiles, and any chatter about Maria. The men promised to ferret out what details they could on her condition and location. Even confirmed sightings and rumors might help piece together an extraction plan.

When talk turned to potential vulnerabilities in Chuck's operation, the otherwise verbose Keegan grew reticent. The other two noticed his sudden discomfort and pressed for insight into the stronghold's most exploitable weak spots. But Keegan withdrew into evasive muttering, refusing to elaborate.

Sam made a mental note of this odd reaction. Clearly there were gaps in what their new partners were willing to divulge. He would work on gaining their full trust in time. For tonight, he decided not to press. Planting the seeds of uprising took cultivation and patience. There would be time to reap a full harvest soon enough.

As the night deepened, the groups reluctantly disbanded after agreeing to a next rendezvous in two nights' time. Sam hung back, speaking privately with Keegan in hushed tones as the others departed separately. Joe cocked his head, trying to make out their conversation. But Sam clammed up on the walk back, only saying he wanted to feel out everyone individually moving forward. Joe had learned not to press the cagey soldier and his unorthodox methods. Results were all that mattered.

Over the next day as they awaited the appointed night, Joe endlessly quizzed Sam for any scrap of useful intel their undercover men passed along. Maria was being kept under close watch in the old records room in the east wing of the city hall building by all accounts. But guards prevented anyone from getting too close, keeping her isolated at Chuck's command.

Sam tried to temper Joe's fervor for planning a risky extraction immediately. "We're just getting our hooks in these boys. Gotta be patient so they keep biting," Sam cautioned. "One dumb move now and we lose our advantage."

Joe reluctantly agreed, though the forced inaction made him feel powerless. He took to sitting alone honing his knife collection to razor sharpness, imagining plunging the blades into Chuck's black heart. If that bastard touched one hair on Maria's head, he would know pain unimaginable before the end.

The night of the arranged meet-up, Joe sent along a thin parcel with Sam, instructing him to pass it secretly to Keegan. The sealed package contained a message for Maria. With luck, Keegan could find a way to slip it to her undetected.

As they waited for Sam and Jake's return, Joe paced and watched the windows anxiously. The message contained a message of hope for Maria. Joe wanted Maria to know he was there and to keep the faith. Somehow, he would manage to get her free. Cryptically worded insurance if things went sideways on their end. It was a risk, but Joe needed Maria to know she wasn't alone in this hellhole. Help was close at hand, plotting her deliverance.

Near dawn, Sam and Jake strode in looking pleased. Keegan had accepted the parcel readily enough with assurances he would get it directly into Maria's hands posthaste. The other men also seemed to be coming more fully into the fold. They agreed to discreetly scout Chuck's central operations room for schematics to share at the next meeting. Even the tight-lipped Boyd was warming up.

"I'd say we've got these boys primed to help spring Maria one way or another if she can play along," Sam said confidently. "Just gotta massage egos and greed a bit more."

For the first time in days, Joe felt a stirring of real hope. Perhaps with allies on both sides they could crack this fortress wide open. Maria just needed to hold on a little longer. It gutted Joe to make her wait even one more day in torment. But they had to be smart, or they would all end up in unmarked graves.

CHAPTER SEVEN
PORTRAITS OF SUFFERING

Maria stared at the cryptic message for the dozenth time. She had found it buried in her mashed potatoes on her dinner plate that was delivered by one of her guards. Struggling to absorb the weight of its meaning. "Help close. Be ready. Details soon. JK"

Joe was somehow here orchestrating her deliverance. Maria didn't know whether to sob in relief or scream in frustration. Chuck had been extremely paranoid in recent days, rattled by whispers of brewing sedition. Her chances for escape dwindled hourly as his paranoia grew. She longed to dash off an answering message telling Joe to flee this cursed place before it was too late.

But such an act would be suicidal. Chuck scrutinized everyone and everything around her now like a jealous lover fearing betrayal. She'd endured degradation already to protect her epiphany that only spreading seeds of dissent from within could dethrone this tyrant.

So, Maria swallowed her primal urge to warn off Joe. Better he believes her to be a helpless maiden awaiting rescue than learn the truth that she moved undetected through town, awakening courage in citizens and guards alike. Let Joe reclaim the lover left waiting. It was a far safer ploy for them both than revealing her true nature - a woman of decisive action.

Maria tore the note into what seemed like a thousand pieces to make sure it was never discovered. In its place bloomed an iron conviction she must be ready for any opening to break the chains Chuck had forged. Joe was coming. She must prepare to run to his arms or die trying. Even if a reunion was not meant to be, Maria refused to cower or lose hope.

The time rapidly approached to end this wicked dominion by any means necessary. Chuck could sense the growing dissent, lashing out more erratically each day. As his irrational violence escalated. Maria was ready to shed her noble pretenses too and take up the sword if it came to that. Her zeal would help kindle a wildfire to purge this rot if they could spark a blaze soon.

Until then, she kept her smoldering fury and true intentions masked, playing the part of an adoring wife waiting dutifully to be reclaimed. From his hidden place, Joe would be laying out his own plans. The combined combustible forces building on both sides could not be contained for much longer. Maria silently urged Joe to hasten. Destiny awaited.

CHAPTER EIGHT
FAMILY TIES

P aulette took a deep breath as she followed her daughter Taylor and the young girl Alicia into the rustic cabin, mentally preparing herself to face figures from her past after so many years away. Sure enough, seated in a rocking chair by the stone fireplace was Toni, her ex-husband Joe's elderly mother.

Toni had been smiling softly down at the toddler playing on the braided rug, but her expression soured the instant she spotted Paulette hovering uncertainly near the door. The older woman's faded blue eyes narrowed, her thin lips pressing into a tight line.

"Well well well, look what the cat dragged in," Toni muttered. "Come to beg for charity from the family you abandoned?"

Paulette winced but supposed she deserved the resentment after walking out on Joe and the kids all those years ago. Smoothing her threadbare traveling clothes self-consciously, she took a cautious step forward.

"It's good to see you again too, Toni," Paulette said, forcing a smile. "How've you been holding up since...well, since everything happened, it's been a long time?"

Toni's pale blue eyes were like chips of ice. "Not long enough, if you ask me," she said bitterly. Toni's sharp gaze raked over Paulette's disheveled appearance. "Better than you from the looks of it," she sniffed dismissively.

An awkward silence followed, broken only by the popping and crackling of the logs in the fireplace. Seeking to ease the tension, Taylor spoke up in a falsely bright tone.

"We were so relieved when Dad, Jojo and Gram made it here safely," Taylor told Paulette, hoisting the giggling toddler onto her hip. "But then they left again right away once they heard..."

Taylor's voice trailed off as she realized Paulette had no context for recent events. Setting Parker down with some wooden blocks, Taylor gave her mother the full backstory - how after the pulse hit

Miami, Joe, Jojo and Toni had battled their way north through rural Florida to make it to the cabin. Dad, only to fall head-over-heels for Maria, a lovely nurse they met along the way.

Maria had been separated from her husband trying to get a divorce from him in Miami when everything went dark, Taylor explained. When they arrived, they quickly found out about this evil man who had taken control of Leesburg and basically had become a dictator. When Maria heard the man's name, it turned out that it was her estranged husband. She felt duty-bound to confront him in their old hometown which had apparently descended into depravity. She slipped out in the middle of the night to go try to reason with him and hopefully stop him. So of course, Dad gathered reinforcements and raced off on a dangerous mission to rescue his new paramour, barely stopping to catch his breath after reaching the relative safety of the cabin.

"That sounds just like Joe," Paulette said with a shake of her head, though privately she was glad to hear her stubborn ex had managed to find love again. She wished him every happiness with this Maria woman, if only they could retrieve her safely.

While Taylor caught her mother up, Alicia had wandered over to the fireplace where Toni sat glowering. The teen gave the older woman a friendly smile.

"So, you must be Joe's mom? I'm Alicia, Paulette's told me so much about your family on our travels here together," the girl said sweetly, perching on the edge of the hearthstone. "It sounds like you've all been on quite an adventure since everything changed. Are you holding up okay?"

Toni eyed Alicia warily but the girl's kindness and concern seemed genuine enough. The elderly woman's expression softened a fraction as she replied, "Well aren't you a polite young thing. I'm still kicking alright, though these old bones don't much care for all this excitement."

She nodded her chin toward where Paulette and Taylor were immersed in hushed conversation across the room. "Can't say I'm thrilled to have that one back under our roof," Toni said bluntly. "But I suppose beggars can't be choosers in times like these. She abandoned my son and grandkids once before. I pray she doesn't cause more heartache."

Alicia nodded solemnly. She understood the older woman's misgivings given Paulette's difficult past. But Alicia also knew firsthand the remorse and desire for redemption that her new friend carried in her heart.

Before the teen could offer any reassurances, heavy footsteps sounded on the front porch, followed by a man's deep voice. "Hello? Is my sister Claire here?"

Taylor rose swiftly. "Stay here, I'll see what this is about." She headed outside.

Paulette tensed, moving instinctively closer to Toni and Alicia. She strained to make out the muffled conversation through the walls. A few minutes later, the front door creaked open.

"It's okay, you can come in," Taylor called behind her.

A tall, bearded man with a stocky build and alert brown eyes stepped inside. He wore tattered jeans and a worn leather jacket. His gaze swept the room before settling on Taylor.

"Name's Miguel. Claire's my little sister. I've been trying to catch up to her for weeks." His voice was gruff but earnest. "Is she here?"

Taylor hesitated only a moment before saying, "No, I'm sorry. Claire went with our group to a town called New Leesburg. It's just a few miles north of here."

Miguel scowled, scrubbing a hand through his dark, tousled hair. "What the hell is she doing there?"

"It's a long story," Taylor said. She summarized the mission to rescue Maria from her abusive husband who'd taken control of New Leesburg. "Claire wanted to help. They left a couple of days ago."

Miguel digested this news with a stormy expression. Then he squared his shoulders. "Right. Looks like I'd better haul ass after them then. My sister's got guts, but she can't take on some damn warlord alone." He nodded curtly at Taylor. "Appreciate you telling me ma'am."

He turned on his heel and strode out, letting the door bang shut behind him.

Taylor stood frozen for a moment, then relaxed and returned to her chair. "Well, that was interesting. At least he seemed decent, if a little intense. Hopefully he catches up to the others in time."

"We can only pray," Paulette murmured. She glanced at Alicia and Toni, taking comfort in their presence.

A weighted silence filled the cabin, each of them lost in their own thoughts and fears for the brave group venturing into the unknown. They could only wait and hope.

CHAPTER NINE
MARIA'S DARING ACT

Maria waited until the dead of night when the lone guard stationed outside her door was most likely to be drowsy and inattentive. She changed into the darkest clothing she could find from what Chuck had left for her and secured her hair in a ponytail. Once dressed, she silently cracked her door open while hugging the wall in a blind spot out of the guard's line of sight.

Her destination was the old city hall basement. Maria suspected female prisoners were being kept locked away there, based on overheard hints from guards. She intended to find proof and hopefully help free those poor captive women if she could manage it.

She could hear the guard's rhythmic breathing and slight snores, indicating he had drifted off as she'd hoped. Inching the door open further, Maria slipped out into the hall, pulling the knob closed behind her with excruciating slowness to avoid any click of the latch waking the guard.

Keeping her back pressed to the wall, Maria sidestepped down the darkened corridor, avoiding any creaky floorboards. The guard continued to doze, oblivious as his charge slid past into the gloom.

At the end of the hall, Maria descended the servants' staircase, keeping to the outer edges where the steps were less likely to creak underfoot. She crept down flight after flight until she reached the basement level of the aged city hall building.

Finally reaching the basement, Maria froze as a loud snore echoed from within. Peering into the gloom, she spotted a dozing guard, slumped in a rickety chair outside the row of cells. Heart pounding, Maria tiptoed past him as she peered into the cells.

Inside she could make out dozens of young women locked in separate cells. They wore dirty, tattered dresses and looked underfed and hollow-eyed beneath the dim swaying lightbulb overhead. Her suspicions were confirmed - Chuck was keeping female prisoners detained in horrific conditions beneath his headquarters.

Maria crouched down, putting her face close

to the bars of the nearest cell. The occupant sat slumped on a dingy cot, not even looking up at Maria's arrival.

"Don't lose hope," Maria whispered urgently. "I'm going to get you all out of this hellhole, I promise."

At Maria's hushed words, the girl's head jerked up, eyes widening. Maria pressed a finger to her lips, then pointed upstairs meaningfully. The prisoner seemed to understand, nodding silently with a glimmer of desperate hope in her sunken eyes.

Footsteps sounded from above, growing louder as they descended the stairs. Maria's blood turned to ice - the guard's replacement was coming to check on the prisoners.

She scanned the basement frantically but there was nowhere to hide.

Heavy boots trampled down the last steps and halted abruptly. Maria cringed as a gruff voice barked out "Hey! Who the hell are you?"

Rough hands seized Maria's hair from behind, spinning her around. She found herself face to face with a burly guard, his scarred features set in a suspicious scowl.

"You ain't allowed down here," he growled, tightening his painful grip on Maria's arms. "How'd you get in here?"

Maria's pulse pounded but she kept her voice steady. "Unhand me at once. I am Maria, the mayor's wife."

The guard's eyebrows shot up. He squinted down at Maria with a new appraisal. "The mayor's old lady, huh?" A crooked grin split his unshaven face. "Guess you got turned around in this gloomy basement."

He released his hold on Maria's arms only to take a firm grip of her elbow instead. "Why don't I escort you back upstairs...Ma'am." The honorific dripped with mocking scorn. "I'm sure your husband is eager for your company."

With that, the guard steered Maria firmly toward the stairs. She cast a desperate glance back at the women watching powerlessly from their cells. Their fate was now in her hands.

Maria considered fighting or crying out for help. But she knew it was useless. She allowed herself to be marched upstairs silently, biding her time.

The guard rapped his knuckles sharply on the door to Chuck's office then shoved Maria inside ahead of him. She stumbled, barely catching herself from falling headlong onto the filthy carpet. Behind his massive desk, Chuck looked up from some paperwork, clearly annoyed by the interruption.

"What's the meaning of this?" Chuck snapped as Maria righted herself. Before the guard could respond, his gaze landed on his disheveled wife. His expression shifted to one of surprise.

"Maria? What's going on here?" Chuck asked in a too-calm voice that immediately put Maria on edge.

The guard eagerly described finding Maria in the basement prison after somehow slipping past her escort upstairs. With each damning detail, Maria could see Chuck's face darkening, even as he maintained an eerie composure.

"Is this true?" he asked softly once the guard finished. "You were nosing around my secured holdings?"

Maria lifted her chin defiantly. "Yes. I discovered your wretched secret prison. What you are doing to those poor young women is appalling!"

Whatever reaction Maria expected, it was not for Chuck to erupt from his chair and stride around the desk to backhand her savagely across the face. The force of the blow knocked Maria to the grimy carpet once more. She cried out in shock, gingerly touching her throbbing, swelling cheek.

Chuck loomed over her; face mottled with rage.

All pretenses were gone. This was the tyrant behind the mask - and he had been betrayed.

"You treacherous bitch!" Chuck roared. "I give you everything! Shelter, protection, access! And this is how you repay me?"

He seemed on the edge of striking her again when Maria scrambled back, holding up a hand to shield herself as she cowered on the floor. Chuck trembled with barely contained fury.

"Lock her in the stockade overnight," he ordered the waiting guard through gritted teeth.

"At dawn, I will show this town what befalls those who dare defy me. My own wife will face execution for her treasonous behavior! Also, whoever was guarding her door upstairs, shoot him in the head and drag his body into the street"

Rough hands seized Maria under the arms, dragging her outside toward the town square. All the fight had left her body. She hung limp and unresisting between the two guards now escorting her to the wooden stocks set up on a raised platform.

The heavy wooden beam came crashing down, locking Maria's bruised wrists and neck in place on the pillory. Bleeding and in agony, she spent the night collapsed there on display under the stars as if in shackles. The tolling of distant church bells marked the long hours until her death at dawn.

* * * * * * * * * * * * * * * * * * *

Within hours, word had spread through New Leesburg of Maria's imminent execution. Most who heard were shocked yet resigned that even the mayor's own wife had defied him and was now condemned. But a few were inspired to hushed discussions of fighting back. Was dissent possible after all?

From a filthy utility shed on the outskirts of town, Claire listened in disbelief as the drifter Keegan described the public shaming of Maria. How she had been locked overnight in the pillory and was set to be executed at first light. They were nearly out of time - Maria's life hung by a thread.

Claire urgently relayed the news to Joe and the others. As expected, Joe became nearly crazed, demanding immediate action to save Maria. But Sam grasped Joe's shoulder, advising restraint.

"Going off half-cocked will only get us all killed, Maria included," Sam said bluntly. "We need to stick to the plan."

Though Joe trembled with the urge for action, he grudgingly conceded the wisdom of waiting.

Their only advantage was the element of surprise. A frontal attack now would fail catastrophically.

Under cover of darkness, Sam set out alone to urgently confer with his inside men, Keegan, Darryl and Boyd. The time had come at last to turn on Chuck and his cronies from within. Only a well-coordinated betrayal and rescue could save Maria from the gallows now.

Sam slipped through the shadows toward the rendezvous point, his hand resting on the revolver tucked in his waistband. Everything hinged on his men being ready and willing to fight when the moment came. Surprise and swift violence of action were the only hope left.

CHAPTER TEN
CHUCK'S RETALIATION

The pale dawn light filtered through the trees, casting flickering shadows on the worn forest path. Miguel strode with determination, his eyes fixed ahead. Finding Claire and the others was his singular focus after weeks of fruitless searching. He moved with the coiled energy of a spring, ready to unleash on anyone who threatened his sister.

Up ahead, the sound of distant voices reached Miguel's ears. He halted, listening intently. The voices seemed to be coming from just off the path up ahead. Miguel proceeded cautiously, one hand resting on the rifle slung across his back. As he drew nearer, he spotted a ramshackle structure tucked back in the trees. The voices were clearer now, strained and urgent.

"...just hope we can get to Maria in time," a gruff voice was saying. "She's set to be executed at sunrise."

Miguel's ears perked up. That had to be Claire's group. Wasting no time, he marched up and rapped his knuckles sharply on the shed door. The murmuring inside cut off abruptly. After a pause, the door creaked open a crack and a pair of hard hazel eyes peered out suspiciously.

"Who the hell are you?" the man demanded. Miguel caught a glimpse of several others crowded inside, watching him warily.

"Name's Miguel. Looking for my sister, Claire," he said briskly. "She with you folks?"

The man's eyes narrowed, looking Miguel up and down. After a moment he gave a curt nod and opened the door wider.

"Yeah, Claire's here. C'mon in."

Miguel stepped inside the dingy shed. In the dimness he spotted Claire looking at him in shock.

"Miguel?! My god, how did you find me?" Claire rushed forward and threw her arms around him. Miguel returned the embrace gruffly.

"I found your note in my cabin and have been tracking you for weeks, sis. You don't cover your tracks for shit," he said, but his tone was affectionate.

Claire gave a choked laugh. "Guess all dad's training paid off." She held her brother at arm's length, relief washing over her. "I'm so glad you're okay."

Miguel's gaze took in the rest of the group - a brawny older man with a salt-and-pepper beard who seemed to be the leader, a thirty-something soldier type, and a lean younger man. They watched the exchange with interest.

Claire quickly made introductions. "This is my brother, Miguel. Mig, meet Joe, Jake and Jojo."

The men exchanged terse nods. Joe crossed his burly arms over his chest. "So, what brings you chasing after Claire, friend?" His flinty eyes bore into Miguel.

"Looking after my little sister. Only family I got left. I made it to your cabin, and I think your daughter Taylor? Told me where you went and what you were up against, thankfully I was able to track you down." Miguel held Joe's scrutinizing stare steadily. After a moment, Joe seemed satisfied. He stuck out a calloused hand that Miguel shook firmly.

"Any kin of Claire's is welcome here," Joe said. "We're grateful for any able hands." He quickly outlined their mission to rescue Joe's newfound love, Maria, from the depraved mayor of New Leesburg.

Miguel listened intently, then cracked his

knuckles. "Happy to help bust some skulls if it means taking down this sick bastard. Just point me where you need me."

Joe clapped Miguel on the back. "Glad to have you, son." He turned to the others. "Alright, let's gear up. We're gonna need our new friend here for the fight ahead."

Everyone began gathering weapons and strapping on body armor in preparation for the assault on New Leesburg. Miguel noted their haggard appearances and meager supplies. This was a ragtag crew, but their determination was obvious. And if Claire trusted these men, that was good enough for him.

As the group finished suiting up for battle, the first rays of sunlight pierced the dingy shed. It was time. Joe gave a sharp nod, and they moved out single file, senses on hyper alert. Miguel brought up the rear, rifle cocked and ready. Up ahead, the crumbling town awaited, along with the deranged man holding Joe's woman captive. Miguel welcomed the fight - protecting Claire always brought out his most ruthless instincts. And he intended to lay waste to anyone who threatened this scrappy new family of hers.

The deserted streets of New Leesburg were

bathed in the warm glow of dawn. Businesses that once bustled now sat vacant, windows shattered, and walls defaced with graffiti. Miguel's sharp eyes continuously scanned their surroundings as the group moved toward the town center. The air was electric with tension, like the rising crackle of energy before a lightning strike.

At the rear of the dilapidated old city hall building, they rendezvoused with Sam's inside men as planned. Sam told them his guys had recruited thirteen more comrades to join in the fight to remove Chuck from power. Miguel noted the undercover rebels shifting nervously as they waited, gripping an array of handguns, knives and tire irons. Hardened men themselves, but fear bubbled beneath their tattooed, unshaven exteriors.

Joe quickly dispersed the expanded crew to their coordinated attack positions surrounding the scaffold that had been erected overnight. Atop its crude wooden platform stood the ominous silhouettes of a noose and stocks where Maria reportedly awaited execution at sunrise for defying the madman in charge. Miguel's pulse quickened at the thought of Claire ending up in her place. This ended now.

Settling into place, Miguel visually mapped

the layout of the square, noting allies and exposed flanks. Satisfied, he peered down his scope and exhaled slowly until the rhythmic thudding of his heart slowed. Calm precision was needed now, not blind rage.

As pale gold light spilled across the square, a hush fell over the scene. Even the pigeons roosting in gutters seemed to sense something momentous approaching. Before long, a large crowd began to gather, shepherded in by Chuck's black-clad guards. The spectators shuffled to their positions with eyes downcast, postures stooped in fear and defeat.

When the first glimpse of color appeared atop the scaffold steps, Joe stiffened like a hound catching a scent. A petite figure was jerked roughly onto the platform between two guards. Her hands were bound and despite a swollen, blackened eye, Maria's proud chin remained lifted in defiance. Joe yearned to rush the platform immediately but clenched his fists and held steady. Timing was everything.

A hush rippled through the crowd as Chuck strode into view. Miguel observed the handsome man with slicked hair and icy blue eyes now addressing the crowd imperiously. So, this was the bastard who would die today. Miguel nestled his cheek against the stock of his rifle, crosshairs trained on Chuck's chest as he awaited the signal.

On Chuck's command, Maria was dragged forth and locked into the waiting stocks. A noose was then lowered around her slender neck. Joe trembled with the urgency to act but kept still as a stone. Their one chance was coordinated execution.

Chuck began loudly condemning Maria as a traitorous harlot, "No one is above the law here in New Leesburg, even my own wife." Chuck exclaimed. "She has been found guilty of treason and must face the consequences. Those that commit treason must face the ultimate penalty, death!"

The first cries of dissent rose tentatively from the weary crowd. One lone voice cried out. "Who found her guilty?"

Chuck began scanning the crowd looking earnestly for the dissenter.

Another voice rose up. "When was her trial?"

Chuck continued scanning the crowd, now looking more unsettled. "She has been judged as guilty."

More voices rose from the crowd, "Judged by who?" "Are you gonna kill us all?" "Where is our food?" "Where is my wife?" "My wife is being used by your men?"

The crowd started pushing closer to the stocks

where Maria was still shackled. Chuck grew more nervous as the crowd grew more raucous and moving closer and closer.

Sensing the simmering outrage, Joe and Sam exchanged a meaningful look. It was time. With a sharp hand signal from Joe, the attack commenced.

A single rifle crack split the air. Chaos erupted in the square as Chuck grasped his shoulder, dark red blood blooming across his pristine white shirt. Miguel quickly shifted his sights, dropping two guards flanking Chuck in rapid succession before they could return fire.

All around, Joe's men vaulted makeshift barricades with weapons drawn, rushing to swarm the scaffold stairs. The crowd who moments before had been passive and cowed now surged forward with a collective roar, emboldened by righteous fury. They tore into the ranks of Chuck's forces like animals unleashed.

Atop the scaffold, Joe roughly cast off Maria's noose then used his knife to slice through her restraints in seconds. Scooping her into his burly arms, Joe bounded down the steps just as the platform was overrun by avenging townsfolk. Together they disappeared into the raging throng.

From his rooftop perch, Miguel provided

cover fire, picking off any remaining guards who attempted to stop the rioting mob. Before long, the square had become a bloodbath as the people unleashed their pent-up rage on Chuck's forces. The tyrant's hold slipped further with each of his loyalists who fell lifeless to the dusty ground below.

When the last of Chuck's men retreated from view, Miguel leaned back from his rifle scope. A grim smile turned up the corner of his mouth. It appeared the town was liberated at last from Chuck's iron grip. Justice had been served this day, along with a healthy portion of vengeance.

Picking his way down through the ransacked central city square, Miguel located Claire and the others as they regrouped. Joe clutched Maria tightly, the petite woman's body wracked with heaving sobs of relief. Even Claire's stoic features had softened into an expression of joy. Seeing his sister safely among friends, Miguel felt the last knot of tension release inside his chest. They had survived against the odds and taken back this community for its people. Whatever came next, they would face together - bonded now like family through the crucible of battle.

* * * * * * * * * * * * * * * * * * *

As everyone regrouped, they began to take a quick headcount to see who was there. Everyone seemed to have made it out of the battle unscathed. Joe, Maria, Jojo, Jake, Sam, Claire, Miguel, Keegan, Darryl and Boyd. Joe asked about the thirteen new recruits that they had gathered. Sam said solemnly "Only eight are here, looks like the other five didn't make it or stayed behind, I don't think we'll ever know for sure."

"Alright everyone, let's mount up and get back to the cabin, we've gotten what we came for." Joe shouted to the others.

"Joe, Maria piped up, "we can't leave now, Chuck got away in all the confusion, he has to be stopped, we can't let him regroup and come back. This has to end right here and now. He was shot and he's wounded, he's now at his weakest"

Joe looked at Maria. "Sweetie, I have you back. We narrowly escaped with our lives, we are the ones who now need to regroup, it's too damn dangerous."

"We can't just let him get away!" Maria said,

her voice edged with anger. "Who knows what that monster will do if we don't stop him now?"

Maria, now wild eyed and filled with resolve, says, "Joe, he has an underground tunnel system that I'm sure he's now using to regain his strength. He's at his weakest right now. We have to crush him now before he can do this all over again. Who here agrees with me?"

Joe looks around the group. "Who here agrees that we need to crush him now?"

Miguel is the first to speak up, "Listen, I don't know you folks very well, but what I saw back there was pretty damn impressive. I say Maria's right, we need to cut off the head of the snake, or he'll be a constant threat."

Joe put his head down, "And the rest of you?"

The group stood silently before Sam stepped up and said, "I tend to agree Joe. He needs to be dealt with."

Maria, sensing the group was leaning her way quickly seized the opportunity to cement her case. "Listen Joe, I get it and I really don't want to go back into the lion's den again, but I think it will be harder if we wait. Plus, Chuck needs to face justice."

Joe, looking defeated, finally relents, "Well, it goes against my gut instincts, we were lucky not to lose anybody today, but I get what you're saying."

Maria continues to solidify her argument. "Joe, there are a lot of people who believe that Hitler didn't die in the Fuhrer Bunker but really escaped using secret tunnels and eventually made it to Argentina to never face justice. Also, that he was planning The Fourth Reich." Maria says, "Now I have no idea if all that is true or not, but I'll be damned if I live with the guilt of letting Chuck get away only to plan his return. I don't want to live with the thought that he could pop up again at any time and start terrorizing people all over again. Joe, I saw things in that town that sickened me, if I didn't at least try to put an end to that man I couldn't live with myself, and besides, that man truly deserves to face the consequences of what he's done to the people of this town.

Joe looked at Maria with a slight smile starting to form across his face, "Wow, I know you wanna win an argument when you start comparing Chuck Warner to Hitler, Joe gave Maria's shoulder a squeeze. "Alright then, I reckon we've got us a manhunt."

Maria sagged against him; relief etched across her face. "Thank you, Joe. You won't regret this, I swear it." He cupped her chin gently. "I hope you're right, darlin'."

As the group starts to organize Maria takes Joe aside for a moment alone together.

She seems to have more on her mind as she stands pensively in front of Joe and looks down at the ground. Joe puts his hand under her chin and lifts her head, "What else is bothering you sweetie?"

Maria looks into Joe's eyes and confesses, "Joe, I uhh, I had to do some things that I uhh."

Joe wrapping his arms around her says "It's ok sweetie, it's ok, you don't have to say anything."

Maria clutches Joe even firmer and says, "I have to tell you everything, I have to get it off my chest, I don't want any ghosts arising later, I don't want any secrets between us, ever. Now is not the right time to go into it, we have work to do, but Joe do know this for now. I didn't think I could ever love anyone as much as I love you and everything I have done since meeting you has been to be with you."

Joe has tears streaming from his eyes. "Maria, whatever happened, I don't care. I'm just happy to have you back in my arms once again and I never want to be separated from you ever again. I love you too Maria, so very, very much. If at some point you want to talk about what happened we can do that, if it unburdens you, I'll listen. If you don't want to talk about it ever again, I can deal with that too. Just promise me one thing, that you'll never leave me again. I was so devastated thinking I might not ever see you again"

Maria also in tears says, "I absolutely promise that Joe, and that is a promise that I intend to keep forever."

Joe leans in and kisses her deeply for a long moment. "As much as I don't want to stop kissing you, we better get back with the others, we've got to come up with a strategy for finding that bastard."

* * * * * * * * * * * * * * * * * * * *

After rejoining the group, Maria, using a stick, starts to sketch out a crude rendering of the town of Leesburg in the dirt. "From my memory of the map of the tunnel system I saw, there are basically four tunnels. There are two that are accessible from under the city hall. One on the north side of the building and one on the south side of the building. I imagine the access must be somewhere in the basement of the building."

Maria, now clearly choked up, continued, "The basement is also where I found cells containing dozens of imprisoned women. I imagine that's where Chuck kept his own private stock of women he would use for his own enjoyment. I recall him referring to them as his "Secured Holdings". He is such a sick man; we have to find him, and we need to make sure those women are freed and cared for."

Joe gazed at the map etched into the dirt. "Ok, so what about the other two tunnels, where are those located?"

Maria's jaw now set with anger continued, "The other two tunnels were underneath banks, but I think they are too far away for him to have gotten to. I believe he would go to the nearest escape hatch he could get to and those would be right under City Hall."

Sam interrupted, "Where do those tunnels lead Maria?"

"The one on the south side leads almost due south towards Dixie Avenue and ends at Venetian Gardens which is right on the shore of Lake Harris. The one on the north side moves northeast and leads to North Blvd very close to Herlong Park, which would give him easy access to Lake Griffin." Maria continued, "It makes sense to get to the water, he might have a boat waiting for him at both locations, once he gets on the water he could go in whatever direction he wanted to and who knows what safe house he might have on either or both of those lakes and could eventually pop out anywhere once he's recuperated from his wounds. Your guess is as good as mine as to which direction he might have gone, it's a crap shoot."

Joe looked thoughtfully, "Damn, if we move towards the wrong lake, he gets away free as a bird. How far are both locations from us here at the City Hall?"

Maria looked back down at her crude map. "I don't know for sure but neither one is very far at all, I'd say certainly no more than a mile for both directions."

Claire stood up and said, "We need to move quickly then before he can get on a boat and slip away, we should probably split up into two groups, one going north, the other south."

"My thoughts exactly Claire." Joe agreed "We already have a pretty good idea of where he might pop out, so let's split up and travel above ground to the two locations and see if we can't find him. He's nursing a wound as well so we might have the advantage of being able to travel faster than he is capable, hopefully we can get to the end of these tunnels before he emerges and greet him with a big surprise."

Claire looks at the group. "By my count we've got eighteen people here, let's split into two groups of nine and get this show on the road. Mig and I will take one group, Maria, you know the town, which is the easiest route to follow for us, so we don't get lost?"

"Definitely the south route", Marie said quickly, "We're on sixth street now, just follow it south all the way to the water. I'm not exactly sure where either of these tunnels emerge, so you'll have to keep your eyes open and search around for him. I say once we're done let's plan on meeting right back here. Don't forget we need to free those women trapped in Chuck's prison."

Joe nodded in agreement, "I like the plan, let's get a move on."

The group quickly divided. Joe, Maria, Jojo, Jake and five others formed the group moving to the north and Lake Griffin, while Claire, Miguel, Sam and the others set out south on sixth street towards Lake Harris.

CHAPTER ELEVEN
SHADOWED SUPPRESSION

C huck gritted his teeth against the searing pain in his shoulder as he staggered away from the chaos erupting behind him. Blood oozed between his fingers clutched over the gunshot wound. The shouts and screams faded into the distance as he ducked into a deserted alleyway, gasping for breath.

Ripping off his shirt, he fashioned a makeshift sling for his bleeding arm. The empty streets meant he'd escaped detection for now. But he had to keep moving. Weapon in hand, Chuck descended into the hidden tunnel entrance, sealing the door behind him. He clicked on a flashlight that he had left there beforehand just in case he ever had to resort to this desperate measure. The narrow passageway was now his only hope of escape.

Trudging through the dank tunnel, Chuck

reflected on how quickly his power had slipped away. Just yesterday he had been the undisputed ruler of this town. The brothels, the food distribution, the supply of liquor and cigarettes - it had all been under his control. He had relished the power and the women it brought him. But the arrival of Maria had changed everything. She had stirred up dissent and unraveled his network of cronies. And now here he was, skulking through this godforsaken tunnel like a rat, his shoulder throbbing relentlessly.

The echo of dripping water and scurrying vermin accompanied Chuck's painful journey through the dank and damp tunnel. His flashlight flickered and died, leaving him in complete darkness. He cursed but continued feeling his way along the cold tunnel walls. Escape was so close. He pictured the boat, waiting for him at the end of the tunnel, he had equipped it with a working motor and plenty of gas, his key to freedom.

A dim light appeared ahead - the end of the tunnel at last. Chuck shuffled faster, gritting through the agony. Almost there. He tripped over an uneven section of rock, crying out as pain lanced through his wound. Clenching his jaw, he pushed himself upright and staggered the last few yards towards the light.

Chuck emerged into hazy morning light at the edge of Lake Harris. A small motorboat bobbed gently in the water nearby, just where he had left it. His ticket out of here. Wasting no time, Chuck cut the mooring rope and yanked the starter cord. The engine sputtered to life, and he steered the boat away from shore just as shouts echoed from the shoreline behind him.

"There he goes!"

"Get him!"

Chuck grimaced against the waves of pain as the boat gained speed, skimming across the shimmering blue water. The lakeside cottage community faded into the distance as he raced towards freedom. He had escaped the mob's clutches for now, but his future remained uncertain. Chuck knew he would need to lay low for a long time before showing his face again. But he was a survivor above all else. One way or another, he would find a way back on top.

The jostling of the small boat aggravated Chuck's wound. Blood continued to seep into the makeshift sling binding his shoulder. He struggled to focus through the dizzying pain.

Just then, the boat's engine sputtered and slowed before cutting out completely.

"No, no, no!" Chuck slammed his good hand

against the outboard motor in frustration. The boat drifted aimlessly as Chuck frantically yanked at the starter cord again and again. But it was no use. The engine was dead.

Glancing back in panic, Chuck saw the distant figures scrambling about on the shoreline desperately searching for any boat they could pursue him in. There were shouts coming from the lakeshore. It wouldn't be long before they came after him.

He had no choice but to abandon the useless boat and continue his escape on foot. Chuck rummaged under the seat and found a small first aid kit. He managed to awkwardly wrap some gauze around his throbbing shoulder wound and take a few painkillers. It would have to do for now.

Peering through the morning mist, Chuck spotted the far lakeshore about half a mile away. He would have to swim for it. Gritting his teeth against the pain, Chuck slipped over the side into the murky water. The cold shocked his system and made his shoulder scream in protest, but he forced himself to start swimming with his one good arm.

Each stroke was agony. Chuck panted and struggled, the opposite shore seeming impossibly far away. But the sounds of shouts behind him spurred him on. He had to make it.

Finally, after what felt like an eternity, Chuck's feet scraped mud and reeds. He had reached the marshy bank. Dragging himself from the water, he collapsed in exhaustion for a few moments before struggling upright and limping into the shelter of the trees beyond the shoreline. He was shivering uncontrollably, but he had made it off the lake.

Chuck plunged into the woods, driven on by adrenaline and fear. He had no clear plan now except to get as much distance as possible between himself and his pursuers. Glancing over his shoulder, he saw figures piling into boats back on the lake. The hunt was on. Chuck cursed and staggered faster through the trees.

The forest provided plenty of cover, but it was rough going. Thorny bushes clawed at Chuck's skin while fallen trees and sinkholes blocked his path repeatedly. He pushed through it all desperately. He came to a small creek swollen with recent rains. Gritting his teeth, Chuck stepped into the surging waters and slowly crossed, using a fallen log for balance. A branch snapped against his injured shoulder, and he cried out, but managed to keep moving.

Finally, the creek opened up into marshlands. Chuck slowed, breath heaving. His shoulder throbbed mercilessly, and he felt feverish and lightheaded from blood loss. The gauze bandage was soaked through. He needed to rest and tend to his wound.

Chuck found a small clearing amongst the trees; it was heavily covered by the tree tops overhead. It would have to do for shelter, at least for a brief time so he could rest. He tore a strip from his pants and used it to re-wrap his shoulder as best he could. Then he huddled in

exhaustion, trying to gather some strength. His predicament was dire. He was a wanted man now, injured and on the run. All his dreams of building his empire had been dashed in an instant.

As the hours passed, Chuck dozed fitfully, clutching his weapon close. Hunger gnawed at his belly, but he had no food or water. Chuck hoped they had given up the search for now. He would have to stay hidden until he regained some strength.

Finally, as the light faded, Chuck knew he had to move. He crept from his makeshift den, body stiff and wound on fire. He needed to find water and real shelter soon. Stumbling through the marshes in the gathering darkness, Chuck eventually came upon a deserted cottage. He approached cautiously; gun drawn. It appeared empty.

Slipping inside, Chuck quickly barricaded the doors and shuttered the windows. He tore through the cupboards, finding some canned food, bottled water and whisky. It wasn't much but would sustain him for now. He wolfed down some cold beans from the can before treating his wound again, washing it with whisky. The alcohol made him yelp in pain, but he hoped it killed any infection. He bound it tighter.

Finally, Chuck allowed his exhausted body some rest, collapsing onto a moth-eaten couch. But sleep was plagued by feverish nightmares of the mob descending upon him again. He was a fugitive now, a shadow of his former self. But Chuck had no intention of going down without a fight. He would find a way to regain power and pay back those who had wronged him. For now though, he just needed time to heal and plot his next move carefully. The game wasn't over yet.

CHAPTER TWELVE
NORTH TO LAKE GRIFFIN

J oe squinted against the glaring sun, surveying the still waters of Lake Griffin. Other than a few ripples from the gentle breeze, the lake was like glass—not a boat or even a bird disturbed its smooth surface.

"Doesn't look like there's much activity here," he remarked over his shoulder to the others.

Maria stepped up beside him, brushing a loose tendril of dark hair from her face. "No sign of Chuck either. Do you think he could be hiding somewhere around the shoreline?"

Joe shrugged his broad shoulders. "Possible. We'd better take a closer look, just in case."

Hefting his rifle, Joe led Maria, Jojo, Jake, and the other five members of their scouting party along the edge of the lake. They all moved cautiously, alert for any movement amongst the trees and underbrush.

so far, their search yielded nothing out of the ordinary.

After two hours with no results, they regrouped by an overturned rowboat half-buried in the mud. Joe swiped an arm across his sweat-dampened brow.

"Doesn't seem like there's much around here. Any ideas?"

Jake, ever the quiet one, simply shook his head. The others murmured and shrugged, just as much at a loss.

Jojo spoke up. "We could try circling the whole lake, see if there's anything on the far side."

Joe considered this but then shook his head. "That would take too long. Our best bet is to—"

"Hey, over here!" One of the scouts called. "I think I found something!"

Everyone hurried over to where the man was brushing dirt and leaves away from what looked like a metal hatch set into the ground. Joe crouched, examining the door.

"Well I'll be damned," he muttered. "This must be the end of the north tunnel from City Hall. Give me a hand clearing this debris."

Together, they exposed the entirety of the large, circular metal door. Joe grabbed the handle and pulled.

Nothing. Maria handed him a thick branch to use as a pry bar and after several forceful tries, the hatch creaked open on protesting hinges.

Joe clicked on his flashlight and shined it down the revealed passage. Concrete steps disappeared into darkness. The air wafting up smelled musty and stale.

"What do you think? Anyone down there?" Maria asked doubtfully.

Joe pursed his lips. "Doesn't look like this place has been used in a long while. But we'd better check it out just to be sure."

One by one, they descended until they stood in what looked to be an abandoned underground bunker. Dust layered every surface, and cobwebs draped the corners. Joe swept his light over a small living area, kitchenette, and several doors leading off to other rooms. All of it silent as a tomb.

"I reckon this place has been abandoned for some time," Joe surmised. He glanced around at the faces of his companions, barely visible in the dim light. "Doesn't seem like Chuck is holed up here after all. We'd best be getting back. The others will be waiting for us at city hall."

Nods and murmurs of assent greeted his declaration. They retreated up the concrete steps, securing the hatch door behind them. As the scouting party hiked back towards town, Joe ruminated over the mysterious bunker. He wondered who had built it originally — the government? A paranoid resident? And why Chuck hadn't already commandeered it for his own use. Too many questions without answers. Hopefully the other scouts had found some promising leads in the south end of town.

CHAPTER THIRTEEN
TREADING DANGEROUS WATERS

C laire shielded her eyes against the glare reflecting off Lake Harris. Despite the unrest spreading across the area, the lake remained picturesque as ever. It was hard to believe the peaceful vista hid anything sinister.

Miguel, Sam, and the rest of their scouting group fanned out along the shore, searching for signs of recent activity. So far, all seemed quiet.

Until Claire spotted movement out on the water. "Hey, look!" She pointed toward a small motorboat rapidly moving away from a tiny dock. A lone man sat in the back; face obscured by the distance and angle of the fleeing craft. As they watched, the boat picked up speed, its engine growling across the tranquil surface.

"Think that could be Chuck?" Sam wondered aloud.

"Maybe. We should try to follow him, see where he's headed," Miguel suggested.

The group hurried to the dock, hoping to find another boat. But the only vessel tied there was a worn rowboat with a pair of oars. Hardly ideal for a high-speed pursuit.

"Damnit, no motor," Claire cursed in frustration. She shielded her eyes again, squinting toward the center of the lake. "Look, his engine must have stalled. He's dead in the water."

Sure enough, the other boat was drifting aimlessly, about halfway across the lake. Its driver was no longer visible.

Sam was already hauling the rowboat into the water. "Come on, we can row out there! Maybe we can reach him before he gets the engine started again."

Claire, Miguel and Sam clambered into the narrow boat. Miguel and Sam took the oars and began straining against the weight of the crashing waves. Slowly, they closed the distance to the stalled boat. Sun sparkled on the water while ripples lapped gently at the wooden hull with each stroke.

When they finally drew within earshot, Claire called out "Hello? Everything okay over there?"

No response came. The motorboat bobbed silently. Claire exchanged an uneasy glance with Miguel. As they pulled alongside, it became obvious the driver was no longer on board.

Sam frowned, leaning to peer over both sides. "Where the hell did he go?"

"You don't think he swam to shore, do you?" asked Miguel dubiously.

Claire shook her head. "That's really far. But he must have escaped somehow." She chewed her lip in consternation. "Either he swam to the far shore or more likely, he drowned trying." The sun reflected off the rippling water was making her eyes ache. "We'd better get back. The others will be wondering what happened to us."

"Yeah." Sam's mouth twisted unhappily. "Doesn't seem like we're gonna catch this guy now."

Resting the oars, Miguel looked thoughtful. "Let's search the boat quickly, see if we can find anything useful."

They spent a few minutes rifling through the scanty contents — life jackets, rope, gas can — but turned up nothing to identify the owner or where he came from. Claire clicked her tongue in annoyance. Another dead end.

The return row to shore was accomplished in dispirited silence. As the hull scraped back onto the dock, Miguel sighed and rubbed the back of his neck.

"Well, I guess that's it here. We might as well start heading for city hall and meet back up with the others."

Claire and Sam voiced their agreement. The group gathered their gear and weapons and set off up the cracked asphalt of 6th street. Claire kept peering over her shoulder, half hoping to catch sight of the mysterious boat driver emerging from some hidden location. But there was no further sign of his whereabouts.

With a frustrated huff, she turned her focus to navigating back through the deserted streets. She really hoped Joe's team had better luck finding some solid intel on Chuck and his operation. Sam fell into step beside her, and she smiled faintly at the soldier.

* * * * * * * * * * * * * * * * * * *

By late afternoon, both scouting groups had reunited in the dilapidated city hall. Joe listened with interest as Claire and Miguel relayed their encounter with the unknown man on Lake Harris.

"Any thoughts on who he might be?" Joe asked.

Miguel shook his head. "No idea. We didn't even get a clear look at him. I suppose he could've been Chuck, but..."

"It's all just speculation at this point," Claire

finished with an irritated huff. "Plus, I have to think if he tried to swim to the opposite shore, well let's just say, I don't give him much of a chance of making it. Especially with a gunshot wound in the shoulder. It just seems to me an impossible task for a guy with that kind of injury, I think he probably drowned out there."

"Well, at least you tried." Joe scrubbed a hand through his salt-and-pepper hair. "Doesn't seem like either of our teams turned up much today. But we need to keep digging."

Maria stepped up and put a sympathetic hand on his arm. "We'll figure it out, Joe. Why don't we take the rest of the night off to recover and let's go free those women in the basement of city hall. Then we can start fresh in the morning?"

The group moved swiftly and silently through the cool, damp dusk toward the looming city hall building. Maria took the lead, anxiety and determination etched into her delicate features. Her hands trembled ever so slightly as she clutched her pistol, knuckles white. Joe placed a steadying hand on her shoulder as they approached the back entrance.

"You can do this," he whispered.

Maria nodded, unable to force words through her constricted throat. She steeled herself and stepped forward, gently turning the door handle. To her immense relief, it opened with ease, unlocked. Chuck's arrogance had made him complacent.

The group filed into a dark, musty corridor illuminated only by the fading day spilling through broken windows. Jojo flipped on a flashlight, the beam cutting through the gloom. They moved cautiously; senses heightened for any signs of guards. But the building appeared deserted, their footfalls echoing eerily off the peeling walls.

At the end of the hall lay a heavy wooden door. Maria pressed her ear against it but heard nothing. She looked back at Joe and the others, heart hammering against her ribs. This was it. With a deep breath, she grasped the handle and pulled.

The door creaked open, revealing a staircase leading down into pitch blackness. The dusty stench of confinement wafted up, mingled with despair. Jojo shone the flashlight down the steps. They descended warily, the darkness swallowing them whole.

At the bottom, the flashlight revealed a long corridor lined with metal doors. The cells. Most had a small, barred window at eye level. Maria rushed to the first, peered inside, and gasped. Huddled on a dirty cot was a painfully thin woman, tangled hair obscuring her face.

"It's okay," Maria whispered. "We're here to free

you."

The woman's head jerked up, eyes wide with shock and disbelief. Maria helped the others open cell after cell, freeing more captive women, each more malnourished than the last. They cringed and shielded their eyes against the flashlights, some too weak to stand without assistance.

As the group aided the frail women from their cells, Maria's heart shattered at the cruel reality of Chuck's tyranny. The most able-bodied women helped support those too feeble to walk unaided. Many wept with gratitude, clasping their rescuers' hands. Others stared vacantly ahead, hollow and broken.

Jojo noticed crude tattoos on their arms, either an A or a B. He recoiled. "That monster branded them like cattle." Fury roiled in his gut.

Once all the cells stood open and empty, Joe addressed the group of women. "You're free now. We have a safe place you can return to with us, if you'd like."

A ripple of whispers and murmurs spread through the group. Several women stepped forward eagerly, but others hung back, shell-shocked and fearful.

One waifish young woman with stringy blond hair spoke up timidly. "My husband - Chuck killed him, took me here. I have nowhere to go." Her voice broke, tears spilling down hollow cheeks.

"You can come with us, dear," Maria said gently, embracing her.

The young woman nodded, lip quivering. Several other widows also agreed to join them after relating similar heartbreaking tales. Jojo's tender heart ached, and he again extended the offer of sanctuary at their cabin.

Some women declined, desperate to search the area for lost children or other family. Joe assured them the door would remain open should they need refuge later.

After accounting for who would be joining their group and who would venture off alone, they scavenged the cells for supplies. Maria and Claire tore sheets and clothing into makeshift satchels to carry what little food and med kits they uncovered.

Finally, the group assembled to rest for a few short hours before dawn's light would summon their departure. Jojo and Sam stood guard at the stairwell entrance while the exhausted women tried vainly to sleep on the cold concrete floor. Maria stared up through the darkness, mind churning. The first rays of sunlight streaming through the broken windows signaled the start of a new chapter, one written by their own hands instead of Chuck's.

As the group emerged from the cellar into the pale dawn, they exchanged resolute nods. The road ahead remained fraught with uncertainty but armed now with righteous purpose. Jojo and Sam took up defensive positions flanking the ragged band of women, who blinked against the muted sunrise as if glimpsing the outside world for the first time.

With cautious optimism, they set off toward home, the cabin their beacon of hope in an ocean of despair.

The journey was excruciatingly slow, the newly freed women could barely move. The plan was to get back to their van and eventually make several trips back and forth to ferry the women back to the safety of their cabin. Several hours into their journey home, the mood in Joe's group remained sober yet hopeful. The women they had liberated slowly regained strength and spirit thanks to finally having access to food and kindly company.

After finally reaching the old van they left hidden in the woods before nightfall, they decided to wait until morning to take the first group of refugees back to the cabin. They would make as many trips the next day as they could before hunkering down for another night. Hopefully they could all be back to the safety of the cabin in just a couple of days. Around the campfire that night, the women opened up about their trauma one halting sentence at a time. Maria and Claire listened with compassion, sharing quietly when glimpses of their own pain surfaced.

One timid young blonde woman spoke up and said her name was Ava. She went on to explain how four of Chuck's men had captured her while she was searching for food. She was held down by three of the men at a time while the fourth violated her and then they would change places. Time after time. They finally brought her to Chuck who had his way with her as well, before putting her with the other women in the prison cells. Jojo listened to her story with tears in his eyes, suddenly he reached out to comfort her with an embrace. Claire, looking on is unexpectedly filled with a jealousy that she can't explain.

Claire tried to push down the unexpected pang of jealousy as she watched Jojo comfort Ava. She knew it was irrational - Ava had just bravely shared her traumatic story and deserved compassion. But something about seeing Jojo's strong arms envelop the pretty young blonde made Claire's stomach twist.

She had no claim over Jojo. They were partners, friends at most. But after everything they'd been through, after relying on each other for survival, she felt a connection to him that went beyond friendship. And if she was being honest with herself, she was attracted to him.

Watching Jojo console Ava stirred up insecurities in Claire that she didn't even know she had. What if Jojo was attracted to Ava? Ava was so petite and feminine. Claire was used to being one of the guys, the tough survivor. She didn't often feel beautiful or desirable.

As the night went on, Claire tried to shake herself out of this jealous funk. It wasn't fair to Ava, who had survived horrors Claire couldn't imagine. And it wasn't fair to Jojo, who was just trying to provide comfort to someone who needed it. But as they settled in for the first watch, Claire couldn't help but feel a little twinge of envy every time she looked over at the pretty blonde curled up asleep under Jojo's blanket.

As Claire and Jojo sat together on watch, she tried to think of something to say to break the uneasy silence that had settled between them. She kept sneaking glances at Jojo, but his gaze was fixed on the dark woods surrounding their makeshift camp.

Claire opened her mouth, then closed it again, unsure of what to say. Just as she finally gathered the courage to speak, Jojo broke the silence.

"Ava's been through hell. I can't even imagine..."

he said quietly.

Claire felt her stomach knot again at the mention of Ava's name. "Yeah," she replied flatly.

Jojo glanced over at her. "You, okay?"

"I'm fine," Claire said tersely.

Jojo studied her face in the firelight. "You sure? You seem...I don't know. Is something bothering you?"

Claire debated opening up to Jojo about the confusing jealousy she felt earlier. But the words stuck in her throat. She was too proud and stubborn to reveal something so vulnerable.

"I said I'm fine," she repeated, her tone making it clear the subject was closed.

Jojo held her gaze for a moment, then nodded. "Okay."

They passed the rest of their watch mostly in silence. Claire's thoughts swirled as she replayed the image of Jojo comforting Ava. She knew she was being unfair, but she couldn't seem to stop the petty feelings of envy.

As the sky lightened with the first hints of dawn, Claire was relieved when it was finally time to wake Maria and Joe for the next watch. She settled into her bedroll, putting her back to Jojo. Sleep did not come easy as she still stewed over her feelings of insecurity.

CHAPTER FOURTEEN
DESPERATE MEASURES

C rouched below the cabin's grimy window, Chuck cautiously peered out at the dirt track leading away through the trees. He had spent the last few days holed up here, recuperating from his injury and evading the bands of armed men scouring the area for him. But he knew he couldn't stay hidden forever. Provisions were running low and the isolated cabin made him feel trapped, like a caged animal awaiting slaughter.

His wounded shoulder still throbbed constantly, a raw, gnawing pain. But the gash was slowly starting to heal thanks to his crude attempts at doctoring it. Chuck had ripped up old clothes for bandages and regularly doused the injury with precious whisky in an effort to ward off infection. So far it seemed to be working.

But he was growing antsy. Inaction did not

come naturally to Chuck. He was accustomed to being a powerful man, in control and calling the shots. Living like a fugitive rat was galling to him. His desire for vengeance smoldered like hot coals in his gut. He wanted to make those that had taken him down pay for their interference, for stealing his world away.

He would rise again, like a phoenix from the ashes. But first he needed to get away, rebuild his strength, and carefully plot his next move.

The morning was quiet, just the chatter of birds punctuating the stillness. Perhaps now was the time to slip away undetected. Chuck gathered his meager supplies - a handgun with a few spare bullets, two cans of beans, a plastic bottle filled with water. It would have to be enough for the journey ahead. He climbed out through a broken window at the back to avoid the obvious trap of the front door. And then he was on his way, moving as stealthily as possible into the dense trees.

Chuck headed south, roughly paralleling the lakeshore. He wanted to put some distance between himself and the area where he had gone into hiding. There were isolated cabins scattered throughout these backwaters and he hoped to stumble upon another where he could rest before continuing his escape.

The terrain was rough going. Dense thickets slowed Chuck's pace to a crawl at times. He skirted bubbling sinkholes camouflaged with vegetation. Occasionally he heard voices in the distance and he would freeze, pulse pounding, until they faded away again. He did not dare light a fire or use a flashlight at night. But he was driven on by determination, putting one foot in front of the other until his body begged for rest.

On the third day, Chuck's perseverance paid off. He came upon a small cabin tucked away in the pines. It appeared unoccupied but he approached cautiously, gun drawn. The door hung crookedly ajar. Chuck swept each room methodically, ready to shoot, but found nothing. The cabin was basic but solidly built, with boarded-up windows. It would suffice as a hideout.

After blocking the door, Chuck inventoried his new domain. The cupboards and pantry were bare except for a bag of rice, some jars of home-canned vegetables, and a bottle of moonshine. He scarfed down the first real meal he'd had in days, then treated his wound again. The swelling and heat had subsided somewhat.

As night fell, Chuck barricaded himself inside

with his gun and meager supplies. He drifted into an uneasy sleep, plagued by memories of his downfall.

Ruthlessness was the only currency that mattered in this world. He would need to be utterly uncompromising to regain his former status and power. All those who had wronged him - the wretched mob that turned on him - they would pay. Chuck would see to it, no matter how long it took. A man like him did not forgive or forget. Any glimmer of mercy in him had long ago withered up and blown away.

* * * * * * * * * * * * * * * * * * * *

Over the next week, Chuck slowly regained some of his strength in the remote forest cabin. His gunshot wound began to heal, leaving behind an ugly, puckered scar. The pain subsided from a constant fiery throb to more of a dull ache. He could use his arm again, although it was weaker than before.

His supplies dwindled rapidly. Chuck attempted some basic hunting and foraging, but with limited success. He snared a few scrawny squirrels in crude traps, and found some wild onions and mushrooms to supplement the last scraps of rice. But it was not nearly enough.

Cabin fever was also setting in. The walls of his cramped hideout seemed to creep closer day by day. Chuck itched to get back out in the world, reclaim his rightful place. He needed followers, weapons, power. Holed up here in the wilderness, he was no better than a feral animal, scrounging and struggling to survive. The itch for vengeance burned under his skin.

Early one morning, Chuck packed his meager supplies and prepared to leave the sanctuary of the cabin. It was time to seek out civilization again, reconnect with his network of allies. He was sure some had remained loyal. They knew the important role he served, bringing order and rules. Without him, chaos would reign once more.

Chuck followed old trapper paths southward through the dense forest. It was slow, grueling travel on foot. His shoes were nearly worn through and his feet ached. But he pushed himself relentlessly until the trees began to thin and open up. In the distance, he heard the unmistakable sounds of a working camp.

As Chuck drew closer, he saw that the noise originated from a makeshift sawmill situated near a fast-flowing river. A group of rugged men were hard at work felling pine trees with handsaws. The mill was converted from an old barn, now housing a saw blade and conveyor belt rigged to process logs.

This was Chuck's first sign of civilization in weeks. Cautiously, he stepped out from the tree line, raising a hand in greeting. The workers paused their labor, eyeing him warily. Chuck cleared his throat.

"My name is Chuck Warner. Just a traveler looking to barter for some supplies."

The foreman, a tall man with a bushy beard, came forward and looked Chuck up and down. "You've got the hungry look of a man on the run. Had some trouble, I take it?"

Chuck hesitated. He needed help but was reluctant to show weakness or vulnerability. "Let's just say I had a difference of opinion with some rather disreputable individuals. Thought it best to remove myself from the situation."

The bearded man nodded slowly. "A familiar story these days. My name's Byron, and this here's my crew." He gestured around at the rough men, their expressions ranging from indifferent to outright suspicious.

"We trade supplies for labor," Byron continued. "You any good with mechanical work? We keep this rig going on spit and grit mostly."

This could be his chance to start over. Chuck nodded. "I know my way around engines decently enough. I'd be obliged for a chance to work."

Byron grinned, showing a couple missing teeth. "That arm give you much trouble? You favor it something fierce."

"I'll work twice as hard to make up for it," Chuck vowed. He didn't mention the nagging ache or how his hand still trembled occasionally when he overexerted himself.

Byron considered a moment, then nodded. "Fair enough. We've got an extra cot in the barn. Meals are communal. Pull your weight and you can stay."

Chuck felt the first stirring of hope. This lumber camp was a far cry from his former empire, but it was a foothold, a beginning. He would gain these men's trust, make himself indispensable. When the time was right, he would start subtly swaying them to his way of thinking, building his sphere of influence once more.

"Thank you kindly," Chuck said with a polite nod. "You won't regret giving me a chance."

Byron waved him over. "Best get started then. Engine's been misfiring something awful..."

The work was backbreaking, but Chuck didn't shirk. He kept the generators and sawmill machinery humming along as best he could despite his limited tools and parts.

The men were gruff but they warmed to him gradually as his clear mechanical chops became apparent.

At night in the barn, Chuck listened quietly as the men exchanged stories over moonshine. He gleaned scraps of news from the surrounding region - tales of unrest, of communities raided by marauders, of disputed leadership. The lawlessness sounded familiar. It seemed civilization remained disordered and fragile post-EMP.

One evening, a newcomer arrived on horseback, a lanky man named Cooper who was a trader peddling homemade liquor. The camp eagerly gathered around, exchanging their scavenged mechanical parts and other wares for jugs of vividly colored booze.

When Cooper heard that Chuck was a mechanic, he mentioned he had some car engines and parts back at his small trading post about 20 miles west in Center Hill. "Stop by sometime...I'd pay decent for a good auto mechanic," he suggested.

Chuck's interest was piqued, though he hid it. Parts meant machines and power. Power meant influence. He filed the information away carefully.

A few days later, a stranger wandered into camp on foot, looking travel-weary with a patched rucksack on his shoulders. Chuck was repairing a saw blade, only half-listening as Byron welcomed the newcomer and offered him a meal. After eating ravenously, the man stood and approached the barn, asking if anyone knew the fastest route west.

That's when the stranger caught sight of Chuck and froze. A look of recognition flashed across his face.

"Never thought I'd run into the likes of you again," he said in a low voice.

Chuck tensed. "Friend, I think you have me mistaken for someone else."

The man stepped closer and whispered. "Don't try your tricks on me. I'd know Chuck Warner anywhere, after what you done to my kin."

Chuck weighed his options, then gestured the man toward the treeline. "Let's talk over here, where we can have some privacy."

Once they were secluded, Chuck turned to face the seething man. "I admit, I've done terrible things. But that man is dead. I'm seeking redemption now through honest work."

The man spat. "Men like you don't change. You deserve worse than death for your sins." He reached for a knife on his belt.

With lightning reflexes, Chuck grabbed the man's wrist, stopping him short. Then he wrenched his arm sharply, breaking it at the elbow. As the man screamed, Chuck snatched the knife and slashed it viciously across his throat. Blood spurted, soaking them both.

Leaving the body hidden under brush, Chuck hurried back to wipe the stains from his clothes and skin. By nightfall he had gathered his belongings and slipped away from the camp, setting out to find Cooper's trading post. He had spilled blood again. There was no redemption for him - only power. This time, he would build his empire on fear and force. None would dare stand against him again.

CHAPTER FIFTEEN
SHUTTLED TO SAFETY

Maria stood guard outside the battered women's camp, shotgun in hand, as the first hints of dawn started to break over the horizon. She peered into the dim morning light, watching for any signs of trouble on the road leading to their makeshift encampment. So far so good, she thought. Hopefully they could get all these poor women moved to the relative safety of the cabin before anyone unsavory discovered their location.

She turned to look over her shoulder at the sound of footsteps approaching. Joe emerged from the shadows, rifle slung over his shoulder.

"How's it looking?" he asked Maria in a hushed voice.

"Quiet for now," Maria replied. "I think we should start waking the ladies soon though. I want to try to get at least two trips done before full light."

Joe nodded. "I'll go grab Sam and get the van loaded up."

As Joe headed off, Maria took a deep breath, mentally preparing for the long day ahead. She tried not to dwell on the horrific stories she'd heard from the battered women the previous night. Right now, she needed to stay focused on the task at hand - getting them all to safety.

She slipped into the camp, moving silently between the sleeping forms bundled up on the ground. Reaching the first woman, she crouched down and gently shook her shoulder.

"Rise and shine," she said softly. "We're going to take a little trip to get you somewhere more comfortable."

The woman's eyes fluttered open, confusion clouding her sleepy gaze. As understanding dawned, her body tensed, fear written across her face.

"It's okay, you're safe," Maria reassured her. "We're taking you someplace safe."

As Maria woke the other women, she saw the same look of anxiety and distrust in their eyes. It pained her, but she understood. After what they had endured, it would take time for them to feel truly secure again.

Outside, the rumble of the van's engine broke the early morning stillness. Joe and Sam had it running and were ready for the first group. Maria helped the women gather their meager belongings and shuffled them towards the waiting van. She noticed tears glistening on a few cheeks, while others stared ahead stoically.

At the van, Sam greeted them with a kind smile. "Morning ladies. I know you're scared, but we're gonna take good care of you. Got a nice place all set up."

The women climbed cautiously into the van. Joe and Maria got the last few settled, then Joe slammed the door shut.

"All right, that's one load," he said. "Get them there safe, Sam."

"You know it," Sam replied, giving a mock salute. Then he pulled out onto the dirt road, beginning the cautious journey to the cabin.

Joe and Maria shared a look, hoping this would be the first of many uneventful trips. There were still so many haunted eyes depending on them.

The rattling of the van fading into the distance left an unnatural silence hanging over the camp. Maria scanned the tree line warily then turned to continue prepping the remaining women for transport. She just wanted this over with, so she could stop imagining all the ways it could go wrong.

CHAPTER SIXTEEN
NEW BEGINNINGS

C huck Warner trudged along the dusty road, his sturdy frame moving steadily despite the ache in his legs and feet. He had been walking for days, putting as much distance between himself and his old life as possible. Now Center Hill was finally in sight.

The trading post came first, a ramshackle building patched together with scrap metal and wood. Chuck stepped inside, blinking to adjust his eyes to the dim interior. The place was crammed with all manner of goods and sundries. Behind the counter stood a broad-shouldered man with a bushy beard. He eyed Chuck with suspicion.

"Help ya find somethin'?" the man asked in a gruff voice.

"Name's Chuck. Just passing through, hoping

to resupply," Chuck said. "I'm looking for a man named Cooper. He told me he's got work for me."

The man grunted. "My name is Harry, supplies'll cost ya. Ain't a charity."

Chuck nodded. His eyes scanned the room, taking in the various shelves, barrels, and stacks. In the far corner he spotted it - an antique diesel generator, the very heart of the trading post. It was sputtering, the telltale sign of a failing fuel pump.

"That your generator?" Chuck asked, nodding towards it. "Sounds like she's struggling."

Harry scowled. "Damn thing's been giving me trouble for weeks. Can't find parts to fix it proper."

Chuck saw his opportunity. He leaned on the counter casually. "As luck would have it, engines are my specialty. Let me take a look, see if I can get her running smooth again."

The big man considered it for a moment before shrugging. "Be my guest. You get it working, I'll let you take whatever supplies you need, within reason."

"Much obliged," Chuck said with a smile. This was perfect. He'd ingratiate himself with Harry and his patrons by getting the trading post's power source up and running again. Food, water, shelter - Chuck needed all of it if he was going to survive out here.

As he popped open the maintenance panel on the generator, Chuck felt the first spark of hope he'd had in a long time. This was a new start for him, a chance to build the life he wanted, a way to build power once again.

Chuck rolled up his sleeves and got to work on the sputtering diesel generator. It was an old but sturdy machine, likely dating back decades. He visually inspected the exterior first, noting the layers of grime and dust that had accumulated. The fuel lines were cracked in places, the belt on the alternator was badly worn. This poor thing had been neglected for far too long.

With a grunt, Chuck hoisted the side panel off, exposing the inner workings. What he saw made him wince. The fuel pump was indeed shot, just as he suspected. The filters were clogged with gunk. But the real problem was the build up of carbon deposits - this engine was long overdue for a proper cleaning.

Chuck dug around until he found some solvents and rags. He started scrubbing away at the years of accumulated filth, revealing the still-sturdy engine block underneath. It was tedious, painstaking work. His knees ached from crouching. His fingers cramped around the stiff brushes. But gradually the generator began to look like new again.

Once he was satisfied with the cleaning, Chuck turned his attention to the damaged parts. The fuel pump was unsalvageable, but he rigged a workaround using rubber tubing and a bicycle pump. It was janky but it would work. The frayed belt just needed a firm splice.

Finally the moment of truth - Chuck flipped the starter switch. The generator sputtered, coughed once, then roared to life. The front section filled with a warm orange glow as the lights flickered on. Chuck let out a whoop of delight. The other patrons glanced over and murmured appreciatively.

Harry clapped Chuck on the back. "Well I'll be damned! Can't believe you got that hunk of junk running again. You've earned yourself a mountain of supplies, friend. And I suspect folks 'round these parts will be knocking on your door anytime something needs fixin' from now on."

Chuck just smiled, basking in his small triumph. This was the fresh start he needed.

CHAPTER SEVENTEEN
SECRETS REVEALED

B ack in the familiar surroundings of Joe's cabin, Maria felt the walls she had built around her past experiences start to crumble. It was here, with the comforting scent of pine and the crackle of the fireplace, that she finally felt safe enough to reveal her secrets to Joe. But even in this sanctuary, her pulse raced with trepidation.

As she sat across from Joe, who had become her confidant and pillar of strength, Maria's hands were clasped tightly in her lap to stop them from shaking. She had come to care for him deeply, and the thought of his judgment or revulsion terrified her.

"Joe," she began, her voice betraying the fear of her vulnerabilities being laid bare, "when I went to confront Chuck... there were things I had to do, decisions I made that I'm not proud of."

Joe watched her with patient eyes, a hint of concern etched into his brow. "I need to know what happened, Maria. No matter what it is, we'll get through it together."

Maria took a steadying breath. "Back at Chuck's stronghold, in order to survive and find a way to fight back, I had to deceive him, make him believe I was with him again, that I supported what he was doing." The words left a bitter taste in her mouth. "I played the role of the devoted wife again, to gather information, to help those girls he held prisoner."

Her voice broke as she continued, the memories flooding back in painful waves. "It was... it was a nightmare, Joe. Pretending to be someone I despised. Chuck... he didn't just share information with me. He... he expected the privileges of a husband," Maria's admission was like a whisper, her shame stark in the silent cabin.

Joe's face darkened, his hands forming fists before he consciously relaxed them. His voice was rasp as he spoke, "You survived, Maria. You did what you had to do to stay alive and to bring down a tyrant. That takes a strength I can't even imagine."

Maria looked up, tears overflowing as she met his gaze.

"It wasn't just about survival, Joe. I... I played

along with his desires in hopes he would slip up, give me more information. And he did, but at what cost?" Her voice cracked under the weight of her own revelation.

Joe stood abruptly and moved around the table. Taking her hands into his, he lifted Maria up to face him. "Listen to me, Maria. You have nothing to be ashamed of. You used the only weapon you had in a situation where most would have crumbled. Chuck was the monster, not you."

Looking into his eyes, Maria searched for any sign of the judgment she feared, but all she saw was warmth, respect, and something that looked a lot like admiration.

"You are the bravest woman I've ever met. The past doesn't define us, it just shapes who we become. And you, Maria Warner, are the strongest person in this room," Joe affirmed.

Maria folded into Joe's embrace, allowing herself to feel the comfort she had been denying herself. In this moment, with her painful secrets spoken and met with unwavering support, she knew their relationship had reached a new depth. They were more than survivors or allies in a chaotic world; they were partners built from trust and fused by hardship.

They stood in silence, holding each other. The fire crackled, an occasional pop breaking the stillness, as the sunlight began to dip below the tree-studded horizon. Outside, the challenges of the world waited, but inside the cabin, Maria and Joe found solace in shared strength and a bond that no secret could ever sever.

* * * * * * * * * * * * * * * * * * * *

The rhythm of the cabin settled into a comforting lullaby as night wrapped its blanket over the forest. Maria and Joe, now quiet in their shared understanding and relief, had drifted to sleep, entwined and peaceful in the dim glow of the fireplace.

Claire sat outside on the porch steps, watching the stars peek out from the purpling sky. The night was cool, with whispers of pine and earth mingling in the air. She inhaled deeply, trying to steel her resolve. The feelings she harbored for Jojo had festered in silence for far too long.

As she wrapped her arms around her knees, the door behind her creaked open. Claire didn't need to look back to know it was Jojo; his presence had become a comfort she could feel.

"Mind if I join you?" Jojo's voice was low, not wanting to break the serenity that night had afforded them.

Claire shifted to make room, but her heart raced as Jojo settled himself beside her, close enough that she could feel the warmth radiating from his body.

"I've been meaning to talk to you about something," Claire began, her voice barely louder than the rustle of the leaves. She didn't meet his eyes, afraid that one look would unravel her completely.

Jojo waited quietly, his gaze patient but fixed on her profile.

"It's about how I've been acting... and feeling, lately," Claire's fingers dug into her jeans, needing something to ground her. "About you."

To her right, she could hear a sharp intake of breath. Abby, who had been walking up to the cabin, stopped, hidden in the shadows by the stairs, listening.

Jojo was still for a moment, a statue crafted from moonlight and concern. "Claire, if there's something on your mind, you know you can tell me. We've been through too much to hold back now."

The silence stretched between them, a bridge Claire feared to cross. Her heart pounded a desperate rhythm against her ribs. "It's just that... I think I feel more for you than just friendship. I tried fighting it because it seemed so impractical. But seeing Ava in your arms made me realize how much..." she trailed off, unable to finish.

There was a stillness so absolute that she wondered if she had shattered something precious. But then Jojo's hand found hers, a touch that spoke volumes.

"Claire, I hadn't let myself hope that you felt the same way. But I've been feeling something too... something more," Jojo confessed, his thumb tracing circles on the back of her hand.

Abby, pressing her body against the rough wooden wall of the cabin, clenched her fists. A tempest of anger, jealousy, and pain was brewing within her. She had harbored an unspoken torch for Jojo herself, a remnant of their past entanglement. Hearing his words felt like a knife twisting deep in her heart.

Claire turned to face him now, her eyes pools of moonlight reflecting his earnest face. "Really?"

Jojo nodded, intense yet gentle. "More than you could know."

Their gazes locked, two solitary souls finding solace in each other. The world narrowed to the space between them, to the soft exhale of their shared breaths. Then Jojo leaned in, closing the gap, and pressed his lips to hers in a kiss that was a promise of tomorrow.

Abby, retreating into the shadows of the night, felt tears burn hot trails down her cheeks. Her anger coiled and snarled, a wounded beast within her. As quiet as the falling dew, she stepped away, her heart dark with thoughts of revenge and the sting of betrayal. Jojo had chosen Claire, and that was a slight Abby could not, would not, let stand unchallenged.

Inside the cabin, as the fire played its dance of shadows and warmth, the new day promised changes and reckonings, for the heart's course was never a simple or painless one. In the peace of the night, Claire and Jojo had found each other, but in the dawn, the path ahead would be wrought with fresh complexities and the echoes of hearts broken along the way.

CHAPTER EIGHTEEN
EVE OF THE AMBUSH

Harry watched as Chuck sauntered around the trading post, chatting amiably with the various traders and merchants who filtered in and out throughout the day. Though he couldn't quite put his finger on it, something about the way Chuck effortlessly ingratiated himself with everyone he spoke to put Harry on edge.

Just yesterday, Chuck had offered to let Harry keep the payment owed for the construction work on the trading post's expansion, if only Harry would allow Chuck to stick around and help run the place. Sweetening the deal, Chuck even offered to provide extra security by living in the back room. Harry had hesitantly agreed with a handshake, but now he wondered if he'd made a mistake.

Chuck seemed to have a knack for drawing out people's woes and frustrations, listening with a sympathetic ear as the traders complained about the difficulty of securing goods and making profitable trades. He'd promise them better days ahead, assuring them that if they worked with him, he could make sure they got what they needed.

It wasn't long before Chuck had charmed his way into overseeing all of the trading post's stock and suppliers. Harry noticed traders starting to come to Chuck instead of him when they needed something. Chuck was also offering expansive credit to those struggling to stock their wares, letting them take supplies without immediate payment.

When Harry confronted Chuck about it, Chuck dismissed his concerns. "I'm just helping our friends out. Don't you want to see the post thrive? Trust me, this will work out."

Uneasy but unwilling to challenge Chuck's authority, Harry said nothing. But over the next few weeks, an alarming pattern emerged. Chuck would give generous credit to select traders, while others seemed unable to acquire the goods they needed, despite Harry knowing they were in stock. Whispers of shortages and long wait times began circulating, though Harry saw with his own eyes that they had plenty of supply.

Chuck was artificially constraining access to

certain goods, Harry realized. By strategically limiting supply and perpetuating the perception of shortages for some while being overly generous with credit to others, Chuck was making himself indispensable. Traders were beholden to him now, dependent on his approval and favors to access inventory.

Meanwhile, Chuck was bleeding the trading post dry with his rampant extensions of credit. Harry had tried to review the books, only to find they were now kept locked in Chuck's office. The few glimpses he caught were alarming - they were hemorrhaging money. But all efforts to raise concerns were met with smooth assurances from Chuck that it was just a temporary cash flow issue, soon to be resolved.

It all came to a head one busy market day, when Harry witnessed Chuck brazenly turn away a loyal trader who had come to collect on a long-standing order. "Sorry my friend, we simply don't have the inventory right now," Chuck lied. Harry saw with his own eyes the ample boxes of the very goods the man sought, stacked and untouched in the back room.

As the distraught trader argued and pleaded his case, Chuck held up a hand. "I'll tell you what. Leave the payment you owe us for now, and I'll see that you get your shipment as soon as it's available."

The man had no choice but to agree. As he walked away, Harry accosted Chuck. "What are you doing? We have his goods - you just don't want him to have them!"

Chuck raised an eyebrow. "Careful, friend. I'm doing what's best for this post. Don't interfere in matters you don't understand." His tone was amicable, but held the hint of a threat.

Harry felt a surge of anger, realizing how much Chuck had taken advantage of his trust. "The best for this post? You're destroying our business! I want you out. Today."

For a brief moment, Chuck's congenial facade cracked. His eyes went cold, and Harry caught a glimpse of the ruthlessness that lay beneath the surface. But then he smiled, an unsettling leer devoid of warmth.

"I don't think so, Harry," he replied calmly. "The traders look to me now. I control the goods. This post needs me." He took a step closer, causing Harry to shrink back involuntarily. "Don't stand in my way. You'll regret it."

Chuck held Harry's gaze with quiet menace before brushing past him to greet a waiting customer. Harry watched with a sinking feeling in his gut. How had he allowed this vipers' nest to form under his own roof?

Over the next week, Chuck tightened his grip even further. He hired some drifters to serve as his muscle, keeping them on as security. Harry found himself barred from accessing stock rooms or financial records - his own trading post was now off limits. Chuck had wrested control completely, reducing Harry to a powerless employee.

Traders knew something was wrong, but Chuck kept them in line with a combination of threats and leverage - no one could afford to lose his favor. Meanwhile, the financial situation grew direr by the day. Chuck was spending lavishly on "loyalty incentives," unconcerned with the consequences. He knew Harry was now helpless to stop the coming crash.

As Harry scrubbed the floor one night, having been relegated to menial janitorial work, he made his plan. If he couldn't reclaim his post, he would make sure Chuck didn't profit from its demise. He would set a trap, make it look like an accident. No one would question a trading post burning down - they lost so much already. By sunrise, all of this would be nothing but ashes and dust. Chuck had won the battle, but Harry was determined to win the war.

* * * * * * * * * * * * * * * * * * * *

Harry crouched in the shadows behind the trading post, waiting for the right moment to strike. In his shaking hands he clutched a can of gasoline and a box of matches, tools he hoped would be the key to finally breaking Chuck Warner's stranglehold on this town.

As Harry steeled his nerves and prepared to douse the wall of the trading post, he was startled by a shout. "Hey! What do you think you're doing?" Harry fumbled the gas can and turned to see one of Chuck's men glaring at him, hand on his holstered pistol. Harry turned to run but the man tackled him, pinning him to the ground. The man grabbed Harry by the scruff of his neck and hauled him to his feet.

"Caught this fella skulking around back with gas and matches," the man called out as they entered the trading post. Harry was shoved to the floor at Chuck Warner's feet. Chuck glowered down at him, his face twisting into a mask of rage.

"So..." Chuck snarled, "A firebug huh, didn't your mother ever teach you not to play with fire?"

He drove his boot into Harry's ribs, who cried out in pain. "I gave you a chance...could have been so easy for you." Another kick to the stomach, and Harry doubled over wheezing.

Chuck grabbed him by the hair and yanked his head up. "But you just couldn't let it go. And now..." In one swift motion Chuck wrapped his meaty hands around Harry's throat, squeezing with all his might. Harry's eyes bulged and his face turned purple as he flailed helplessly. With a sickening crack, his movements slowed then stopped. Chuck held on a few more moments, ensuring the job was done.

Finally he released his grip and Harry's lifeless body slumped to the floor. Chuck straightened his shirt, the rage gone from his face as quickly as it came. He turned to his man with an air of nonchalance. "Get rid of the body. Dump it in the ravine, deep enough no one will find it." The man nodded and began dragging Harry's corpse out the back.

Chuck watched him go with a faint smile. He had eliminated the last remaining resistance to his plans. With Harry gone, no one would dare challenge him again. Soon Chuck would have total control over this entire area. He strolled to his office whistling, already envisioning the empire he would build.

CHAPTER NINETEEN
JOJO'S DILEMMA

S am and Jake trudged wearily up the gravel driveway to the cabin, their packs laden with the meager supplies they'd managed to scrounge up on their latest scavenging mission. It had been a long day spent combing the ruins of abandoned homes and stores, all while trying to avoid the roving gangs that now claimed the streets. They were exhausted, but even these modest finds would help see the family through another week.

As Sam pushed open the cabin door, he was greeted by the savory aroma of a rabbit stew simmering over the fire. Claire stood at the stove, wooden spoon in hand, while Jojo sat at the table cleaning his rifle. Their eyes met for a brief moment before Claire turned her attention back to the pot, a hint of a smile playing at her lips.

Ever since confessing their feelings for one

another, Jojo and Claire had agreed to keep their blossoming relationship secret for now. There were already enough tensions within the family's newly formed survival group without adding an interpersonal dynamic into the mix. But stolen glances and subtle touches told the story their words did not share.

Abby sat in the corner, watching it all unfold. She hadn't missed the furtive exchange between Jojo and Claire. Abby still harbored feelings for Jojo from their past tryst, though she knew he was a different man now - more hardened by the world's harsh new realities. Still, she was determined to come between them, to sow seeds of jealousy and doubt until it drove them apart.

As Sam and Jake wearily shed their gear, Abby sprang up to help unload their packs, making sure to "accidentally" brush against Jojo in the process. "You boys must be exhausted after being out all day," she purred, running a hand along Jojo's arm. "Come sit and take a load off."

Claire's eyes narrowed, but she bit her tongue and busied herself at the stove. Jojo gently extracted himself from Abby's grasp and took a seat at the table.

"Any luck out there today?" Jojo asked Sam,

trying to steer the conversation to more practical matters. But Abby wouldn't relent, leaning in close over Jojo's shoulder as he inspected his rifle.

"I don't know how you boys do it, going out day after day," she said with dramatic flair, letting out an affected sigh. "It's just so dangerous beyond these walls. But I suppose someone has to keep us fed and protected. I feel so safe knowing brave men like you are looking out for us."

As she spoke, Abby shot a sly glance at Claire, looking for any reaction. But Claire kept her face impassive as she silently ladled the rabbit stew into bowls and passed them around the table, saving Jojo for last.

Their eyes met again briefly as she set the bowl before him, a subtle intimacy passing between them. "You must be hungry after the long day," Claire said. "Make sure to keep up your strength."

Jojo gave her a grateful smile before turning his attention to the meal. Abby fumed inwardly at this quiet yet undeniable connection. As the others ate, she vowed to continue her machinations until Jojo was hers once more.

* * * * * * * * * * * * * * * * * *

As Sam ate he turned to Jojo and asked "Bones where's you dad, we need to talk?" Claire said "He's out back I'll go get him for you."

Claire and Joe return a few moments later, Joe asking "What's up Sam?" Sam tells Joe and the others that while scavenging today we ran into a group of people that turned out to be pretty friendly. They told us about a trading post that is operating in Center Hill about twenty miles from here. Joe smiling says "That sounds promising." Sam continued "Maybe, but maybe not." Joe asks, "Why is that Sam?" Sam continues. "The group told us that it used to be a great place for supplies, it was run by an old guy named Harry who traded very fairly with everyone in town." Joe says. "And now?" Sam goes on and explains that Harry has now mysteriously disappeared and the place is now being run by a guy that took over and basically has the town beholden to him and his cronies. They withhold much needed supplies for exorbitant prices. Joe frowns "Too bad, that could've been a great resource, I guess we know not to bother to deal with them." Sam's face hardens. "Joe, that's not all."

Joe froze, fork halfway to his mouth. "What else?"

Sam leaned forward, lowering his voice. "The new man in charge, his name is Chuck."

"Chuck?" Joe repeated in disbelief. "Not Chuck Warner?"

"Not sure, but it certainly fits his MO" Sam nodded grimly.

Chuck cutting rations, hoarding goods, threatening anyone who complains. The man was ruthless and self-serving. If he was running the trading post now, that spelled trouble.

"What's our play here?" Sam asked. "Do we steer clear or check it out?"

Claire and Jojo exchanged uneasy glances but remained silent, deferring to Joe. He stared into the fire, jaw tightening. After a long moment, he looked up.

"We go," Joe said firmly. "But cautiously. I want eyes on Chuck, see what he's up to. We'll scope it out, gather intel if we can. But no direct contact." His tone left no room for argument.

Sam nodded. "Copy that. Recon mission only."

"I don't like it Dad," Jojo said quietly. "Chuck's dangerous."

Joe put a hand on his son's shoulder. "I know. But we need more information. If it is indeed Chuck Warner he won't just stay hunkered down in that trading post. A man like him...if he's setting up shop, expanding his reach...we need to know. Twenty miles away is too close for comfort"

Jojo pressed his lips together but didn't argue further. They had tangled with Chuck before and knew the fallout when men like him seized control. This changed things. For better or worse, their course was set. They would soon be paying a visit to Center Hill.

CHAPTER TWENTY
ASSAULT ON CENTER HILL

Chuck had made himself comfortable in Harry's old office at the trading post, elbows on the desk as his mind worked through his plans for expansion. He couldn't shake off the sensation gnawing at the edges of his ambitions, the desire for more control, more influence... more power. The city under him was ripe for the picking, and he craved to sink his teeth deeper into its resources.

Amidst piles of inventories and transaction ledgers, a particular thought took root – the essential lifeline that could solidify his grip on the town's morale and obedience: liquor. And the man he sought, the key to this venture, conveniently came to mind: Cooper.

Chuck let a slow, sinister smile creep across his face as he recalled their earlier interaction. Cooper had been eager to hire him once, but now the tables had turned. Now it was Chuck who needed something, and the time had come for Cooper to provide.

Enlisting a group of his most loyal and intimidating men, Chuck set out to find Cooper's homestead, a modest farmhouse sitting on a stretch of fertile land where the stills hid among the sprawling greenery.

Cooper saw them coming from a distance, weighing the heavy steel of his shotgun in his hands with an increasing unease that settled cold in his chest. His wife, Terri, peeked through the windows, her breath hitching at the sight of the hazardous procession drawing near.

"Cooper!" Chuck's voice boomed as he and his men approached the farmhouse, their presence alone a looming threat more potent than any spoken word. "We have business, you and I."

Cooper stepped out onto the wooden porch, mustering as much fortitude as his voice could carry. "Chuck. What brings you out here?" The words felt weak even to his own ears.

Chuck sauntered closer, a predator baring his teeth in a conversational gesture. "I'm looking to expand my… provisions. And I've heard you've got a fine touch with the stills."

Cooper's gaze flickered over to Terri's fluttering shadow behind the drapes. His resolve hardened. "The stills are mine," he said, defiance etched into the lines of his face. "They ain't for sale."

Chuck's glare slashed at the words, obliterating their weight. "Oh, I'm not looking to buy. No, Cooper. I'm looking to… acquire," he emphasized with malice.

Terri, slender and pale as fresh milk against the backdrop of her darkening kitchen, watched on with terror-stricken eyes as her sanctuary became a stage for wolves.

Cooper clenched his fists, the stubble on his jawline sharper for the anger brewing within. But as Chuck's men fanned out, any arguments he was prepared to put forth withered like dead leaves under the scorching sun.

And then it was Terri's timid voice that broke the oppressive silence, "Cooper, just... let them have what they want." Her plea was a whispered knife, drawing blood from her husband's pride.

Chuck's smile at that moment was that of a man who had already pocketed victory, sending chills racing down Cooper's spine. The stills would go to Chuck, along with the sway of liquor over the town, the key to loosen tongues and open wallets, the lubricant of his looming authority.

As he turned to leave, Chuck's eyes landed on Terri once more, this time unabashed in his appraisal. "You have quite the touch here, Terri. All this," he gestured around the farmhouse, "under your delicate hand. Perhaps we'll discuss how you might serve the community further."

Cooper burned at the insinuation, his hands shaking as he tried to maintain a composed exterior. But in that look, the descent of his world was sealed. Chuck had come for his stills and inadvertently revealed his intent for something far darker, a vice that clawed even deeper at the town's soul.

Chuck departed with a gloat woven into his stride, leaving Cooper and Terri to tend to their wounds and the crumbling remnants of their peace. Chuck now had liquor and the groundwork for his nefarious new network laid bare. His kingdom was taking shape, as were the shadows it cast.

CHAPTER TWENTY ONE
THE PRECARIOUS PLAN

The morning mist clung to the windows of the cabin as Joe, Jojo, Sam, and Jake gathered around the weathered oak table, maps and notes strewn before them. They hunched over the details, plotting, their conversation a murmur against the crackle of the fire.

"We need to know for sure," Joe insisted, his finger jabbing towards the blotch on the map where Center Hill was marked. "If that scumbag Chuck Warner's taken over, we can't just sit back. We find out, then we plan."

Jojo nodded in agreement, leaning back in his chair with a thoughtful expression. "We've got to be smart about this, use the van to get close, but not too close. Park on the outskirts and go in on foot. We stay low, we stay quiet."

"Stealth's our best friend here," Sam added,

pocketing his knife after using it to point to a back road that led to the outskirts of Center Hill. "We can cover ground and get a good view without raising any alarms."

Jake had been quiet, his eyes scanning the layout of the area. "If we follow this ridge here," he said, tracing a line with his finger, "we'll have a good vantage point over the trading post. Nobody should see us."

The plan set, they gathered their supplies, double-checking their equipment. Every step had to be precise; every movement calculated. They were heading into a viper's nest, after all.

The van's engine hummed a low tune as the landscape of trees and underbrush blurred past them. Joe kept his hands steady on the wheel, his vision razor-sharp. They all shared an unsettling awareness that each mile drew them closer to the web spun by Chuck Warner.

The air was thick with tension as they parked in a dense copse of trees, the van concealed from passing eyes. The quartet stepped out, exchanging nods. Without a word, they began the trek towards the heart of Center Hill, moving with the silence and agility of hunters stalking prey.

As the four men crept closer to the edge of the

town, the trading post came into view—a chaotic dance of bartering, the exchange of goods and services, and occasionally, disputes. They watched from their hidden hillside perch as townspeople approached the post with hopeful weariness, looking for fair trade.

From their concealed position, they witnessed the heavy hand of leadership. Chuck's goons patrolled the area, flexing muscle and instilling fear with their brusque treatment of the traders. The air was thick with dissatisfaction and silent anger among the townspeople.

Then, like a dark cloud shadowing the sun, he appeared. Chuck Warner stepped out to oversee his empire of control and extortion, his presence commanding and threatening. He barked orders at his men, his voice cutting through the murmur of the crowd, his laughter a discordant caw above the din.

Joe's fists clenched at the sight, fury boiling in his veins. He watched as Chuck intimidated a young family, their cart of goods spilling as they were manhandled aside. It was the same old Chuck, brutal and callous.

"Easy, Pops." Jojo's voice was steady, his hand resting on his father's shoulder. "We need to keep our heads. He'll get his, but only if we're smart."

The reluctant agreement hung heavy in the air. They had seen enough. With a collective, silent vow of retribution, they took one last look at the trading post before turning to make their way back to the van. It was time to decide how to handle the serpent in their midst—the calculating Chuck Warner.

* * * * * * * * * * * * * * * * * * * *

The familiar silhouette of the cabin materialized amongst the trees, beckoning the returning group with promises of refuge and warmth. As the old van sputtered to a halt in its usual spot, each member let out a quiet sigh—relief and tiredness colliding. The reconnaissance mission to Center Hill had been grueling but crucial. They had needed to know the truth.

Joe was the first to disembark, his boots crunching on the gravel as his eyes scanned the surrounding woods, ever protective, ever vigilant. The rest followed, stretching and shaking off the stiffness from the long drive. Maria, helping to unpack some of the supplies, looked up to catch Joe's gaze, an unspoken question lurking within it.

"Maria, can I talk to you?" Joe's voice was low enough that the nearby chatter of unloading supplies drowned it out.

Maria stepped aside with him, withdrawing from the group. A knot formed in her stomach. Joe had that look—the one that seemed to bear the weight of the world. With gentle concern, she asked, "What's happened?"

Joe took a deep breath, hands on his hips. "We found Chuck," he said, the words heavy and hard.

Maria's heart skipped a beat. "Are you sure?"

"Yes. He's taken over the trading post, roughing up the townsfolk, playing king." Joe looked her deep in her eyes, gauging her reaction. "I wanted to be certain it was him before I told you. This changes things."

Maria nodded solemnly, her mind racing with the myriad of threats Chuck's presence could entail. Her resolve hardened. "We'll deal with him. Thank you for telling me, Joe."

Their private moment was interrupted when Abby, sunning herself on the cabin's lawn in a skimpy bikini, caught sight of Jojo's return. Her face lit up despite her sun-soaked languor, and she quickly launched herself at him, wrapping her arms around his broad frame in a hug that was far too intimate for Claire's comfort.

From inside, Claire watched the enthusiastic greeting with a tightening jaw. The sense of deja vu infuriated her but before she could intervene, Abby was pulling Jojo toward the balcony.

"Come on, let's go out back," Abby said with a flirtatious giggle that reached Claire's ears—and stung.

On the balcony, Abby continued her charm offensive, arms locked around Jojo. But something in him resisted, something that had changed since their time together. With firm resolve, Jojo detached from her embrace. "Stop, Abby. It's over between us," he said, his voice laced with finality.

Abby's eyes welled up with crocodile tears, but the desperation they masked was real. "How can you do this to me, Jojo? After everything..."

Jojo shook his head. "It won't work this time, Abby. We're done. You need to accept it." And with that, he turned on his heel and walked back inside, leaving Abby alone, her emotions a whirlwind of humiliation and brewing anger.

As Abby stood stunned and silent on the balcony, something venomous twisted inside her—a need for revenge and validation. She refused to be discarded, to be ignored. An idea crawled into her thoughts, dark and insidious as nightfall. She knew of a man, a man who was used to taking what he wanted. Chuck Warner.

A sly smile crept onto Abby's face as she allowed her thoughts to unravel into a plan. It was perfect. She was confident Chuck would have more use for her charms than the dismissive Jojo ever did. And she had valuable information to offer — a bargaining chip. With one last furtive glance at the cabin, Abby's decision solidified in her heart. She'd make her way to Center Hill and right into Chuck Warner's waiting arms.

* * * * * * * * * * * * * * * * * * *

The sun beat down relentlessly as the ragtag group of survivors gathered in front of Joe's cabin, their faces etched with worry and apprehension. Joe stood before them, his expression grim as he prepared to deliver the troubling news about Chuck Warner and his burgeoning empire.

"I know you're all scared about what's been happening," Joe began, his gruff voice tinged with empathy. "Believe me, learning that Chuck has seized control of the county, with aims to expand further, shook me too."

At the mention of Chuck's name, several of the women who had escaped his compound shuddered, fresh tears spilling down their cheeks. The horrors they had endured at the hands of Chuck and his men still haunted them.

"We have to decide what to do about this," Joe continued. "Chuck's already hurt too many people. If we don't act, he'll only grow stronger."

The group looked amongst themselves uneasily. Miguel stepped forward, his expression stoic. "I say we take Chuck out, before it's too late. We can't let him keep terrorizing people." Several murmurs of agreement followed his statement.

On the edge of the group, Abby listened intently, her shapely figure draped in a skimpy sundress despite the practical attire of the other women. A sly smile tugged at her lips as she mentally cataloged everything being discussed. This could prove very useful for her own dealings with Chuck...

The debate wore on for hours under the baking sun. Some argued for diplomacy, but the consensus ultimately tilted in favor of decisive action. By late afternoon, a decision had been reached - they would launch a coordinated attack on Chuck's compound, relying on the military expertise of Joe, Jojo, Miguel,

Sam, and Jake to strategize a plan.

As the meeting drew to a close, Miguel stepped forward, his scarred face set with determination. "My friends, this won't be easy. But it's the right thing to do. Chuck's tyranny ends now."

With their course set, the group disbanded to begin preparations. They all understood the gravity of what lay ahead, but also knew that stopping Chuck once and for all was a cause worth fighting for. The time had come to reclaim their futures.

* * * * * * * * * * * * * * * * * *

The group gathered around the weathered picnic table in the front yard, the late afternoon sun casting long shadows across the grass. Joe sat at the head of the table, his brow furrowed in concentration as he listened to the others. To his right sat Jojo and Miguel, their faces somber. Across from them were Sam, Claire, and Jake, while Abby lingered on the fringes, arms crossed as she took in the discussion.

"Alright, let's go over the plan again," Joe said, his gravelly voice low. "Last time, in Leesburg, we almost had Chuck. The ambush worked, we got the jump on him and his crew. But we didn't contain them, and that slippery snake managed to get away in the chaos."

Jojo nodded, his jaw clenched. "We can't let that happen again. If we get him cornered, we need to finish it."

Miguel leaned forward, forearms on the table. "I agree. But we also can't go rushing in without knowing exactly what we're up against. We need intel."

"That's our advantage," Claire offered. "Chuck doesn't know any of us. We can move freely around Center Hill, scope out his operations. Get a feel for his strengths, and more importantly, his weaknesses."

Jake rubbed his chin thoughtfully. "We should also talk to the townspeople, see if any of them might join us. It's their home too, after all."

"Good thinking," Joe said. "Maybe we can turn some of Chuck's own men against him, like we did in Leesburg. Money only buys so much loyalty."

Sam nodded. "While we're at it, we should look for opportunities to disrupt his operations. Small acts of sabotage could go a long way."

Joe agreed, "Let's take the next couple of weeks to gather our gear and solidify this plan completely. I don't want this bastard slipping through our grasp again. We all have too much to lose."

They continued discussing strategy, unaware that Abby had subtly drifted away from the group. As they talked, she slipped into the house and gathered a few essential items. Under the cover of darkness, she would make her way to Center Hill, bringing all she had learned to Chuck. The secrets shared around that picnic table would serve her well in ingratiating herself with the new power in town.

* * * * * * * * * * * * * * * * * * * *

The following morning Jojo walked into the kitchen, the smell of sizzling bacon and brewing coffee pulling him from his slumber. He rubbed the sleep from his eyes and grabbed a steaming mug.

"Morning," Taylor said over her shoulder as she tended to the pans on the stove. "I heard there was quite the scene yesterday with you and Abby."

Jojo scoffed. "That's putting it lightly. She ambushed me down by the lake, prancing around in next to nothing trying to get my attention." He took a long sip of coffee. "I finally had to spell it out clear as day that it's over between us and has been for a long time now."

Taylor lowered her voice. "Good for you,

standing up to her like that. But were you completely honest about why you want nothing to do with her anymore?"

Jojo raised an eyebrow. "What do you mean?"

"Maybe the reason you were so blunt is because you've set your sights on someone new," Taylor said with a knowing smile.

"Maybe," Jojo said, unable to hide his own smirk.

"Yeah, I thought so. And I think she feels the same way about you. I can see it in the way she looks at you."

Jojo sighed. "You're right. Claire and I have talked about our feelings. But with Abby making life hell for us both, we didn't want anyone to know yet."

He glanced around before continuing in a hushed tone. "Just keep this between us for now, okay? Claire and I want a little time before going public. And..." He laughed softly. "I'm terrified of Miguel's reaction when he finds out. Pretty sure he won't take the news well, as protective as he is of his little sister."

Taylor laughed. "Don't worry, my lips are sealed." She turned back to the sizzling pans. "But you should know, whatever happens, I've got your back."

Jojo smiled, gratitude welling up inside him. Even though he and Taylor had fought like cats and dogs growing up, they were always there for each other when the chips were down. With Taylor on his side, he felt like he could face anything.

Jojo was tending to the sizzling pans when Taylor asked, "Isn't it Abby's morning to help with breakfast?"

Jojo frowned, not eager to deal with her after yesterday's drama. "Yeah, it is. I'll go find her." He paused. "Actually, why don't I watch the stove and you go get her? I really don't want to deal with Abby right now."

Taylor nodded in agreement and headed off to find their errant housemate.

Joe and Miguel soon joined Jojo in the kitchen, grabbing mugs of coffee. "Morning," Joe grunted. "Where's Taylor?"

"It's Abby's turn to help with breakfast but she's AWOL," Jojo explained. "Taylor went to track her down."

The three men talked casually about their plans for the day, keeping an eye on the pans. After about ten minutes with no sign of the women, they grew concerned.

Finally Taylor returned, worry etched on her

face. "Abby's nowhere to be found. I checked all over - she's gone."

Alarmed, the group immediately fanned out to search the property. Thirty fruitless minutes later, they reconvened.

"I checked her room and it looks like some of her stuff is missing," Jojo said. "I think she might have actually left."

Just then, Claire walked into the kitchen, looking unbothered. "Well good riddance if you ask me. Hopefully she stays gone for good this time."

Joe scratched his beard, clearly troubled. "I don't like this one bit. It's not safe out there alone. Why would she just up and leave without a word, and where could she possibly go?"

Jojo and Claire exchanged a quick, knowing glance that did not go unnoticed. There was more to this story than either of them were letting on.

* * * * * * * * * * * * * * * * * *

Abby slipped out of the cabin just before dawn, the faint light providing barely enough illumination for her to see the gravel driveway. She had packed light, bringing only a small backpack with some food, water, and basic supplies. The less she carried, the faster she could pedal. Freedom was waiting 20 miles down the road in Center Hill, along with her ticket to a better life - Chuck Warner.

She quietly wheeled one of the bicycles propped against the cabin wall, wincing as the tires crunched on the gravel. Pausing, she glanced back nervously, afraid the sound would alert the others. But the cabin remained still, its occupants lost in sleep.

Satisfied that her escape had gone unnoticed, Abby swung her leg over the bike and began pedaling down the roadway. The cool morning air bit at her cheeks as she navigated the bumpy path. She ignored the discomfort, focusing instead on the future she would build with Chuck once she arrived in Center Hill. A sly smile crossed her face as she imagined how shocked the others would be when they realized she had outsmarted them.

Miles passed as the morning sun rose higher in the sky. Abby's breath grew ragged and her muscles burned from exertion, but she pushed harder, fueled by thoughts of revenge. By mid-afternoon, she spotted a battered sign announcing Center Hill ten miles away. "half-way there," she panted, standing on the pedals for more power.

The sun was sinking low on the horizon

when the search party returned to the cabin, their footsteps heavy with failure. One by one they filed into the living room, shoulders slumped in defeat. Joe sank into the worn leather armchair, kneading his temples with calloused fingers.

"Any sign of her?" he asked, though the answer was clear on their faces.

Jojo shook his head. "I checked the south road all the way to the creek. No trace."

"She wasn't down by the lake either," Miguel added. "Or on any of the trails leading out from it."

Jake sighed, running a hand through his tousled hair. "I walked the train tracks east for miles. If she went that way, she's long gone now."

Sam clenched his jaw, anger simmering in his eyes. "We should never have let her stay here. I knew she couldn't be trusted."

"Now hold on," Joe said. "We don't know she's done anything wrong. Maybe she just went for a walk and got hurt or lost." But the doubt in his voice betrayed his true feelings.

Just then, Claire entered the room, her brow furrowed with concern. "Has anyone seen the green bike, the one we found abandoned on Route 6? I just went to check on it and it's gone."

The group exchanged uneasy glances as the

reality set in. Abby had fled, making a clean escape under the cover of darkness. Joe slammed his fist against the armrest. After all they had done for her, this was how she repaid them. But anger quickly turned to worry as he imagined her out there alone as night fell.

"Alright, no use dwelling on it now," he finally said, rising to his feet. "First light tomorrow we'll pick up the search. With any luck, we'll find her before she gets too far."

But as the weary group dispersed, a dark foreboding hung in the air. Something told them this was only the beginning. Abby was out there now, beyond their help or protection. And there was no telling what trouble she might stir up next.

Later Jojo found Claire down by the lake, her blonde hair blowing in the breeze as she skipped stones across the glassy surface. He took a deep breath as he approached, dreading the conversation ahead.

"Hey," he said, his voice strained. Claire turned, surprise flickering across her face. "Can we talk for a minute?"

She nodded, dusting the dirt from her hands. "What's up?"

Jojo shifted his weight, shoving his hands in his

pockets. "It's about what happened yesterday. With Abby."

Claire's expression darkened. "What about it?" Though her tone was neutral, Jojo detected the edge beneath it.

"I should have told you sooner. But she cornered me outside the shed and started getting...physical. I pushed her away and told her I wasn't interested, that it was over between us."

Claire crossed her arms, her jaw tight. "Is that all that happened?"

"Yes, I swear it," Jojo insisted. "Nothing more. But she didn't take it well. Said I'd regret turning her down." He shook his head, regret etched on his face. "I think that's why she took off, she was just lashing out cause she felt rejected."

Claire studied the ground for a moment before meeting his gaze. "We should tell your dad. Keeping this secret is only going to cause more trouble down the line."

Jojo nodded. She was right. Secrets had nearly torn this family apart before; he wouldn't make that mistake again. "Okay, let's go do this."

They found Joe cleaning his rifle on the porch, focused intently on the task. He glanced up as they approached, immediately sensing something amiss.

Jojo hesitated. This wasn't going to be easy. But he had to trust his dad would understand.

"I need to tell you something," he began. Slowly but surely, the whole story came tumbling out - the confrontation with Abby, her attempted seduction, the bitter rejection that must have motivated her disappearance.

When he finished, he braced himself for Joe's reaction. But his dad merely set down his cleaning kit, brow furrowed in thought.

"I appreciate you telling me the truth," he said finally. "And I believe you handled it properly. Abby's always had a knack for stirring up drama." He shook his head. "We gave her the benefit of the doubt, but seems she hasn't changed. Probably best she moved on 'fore she caused more trouble around here."

Jojo released a deep breath, relieved to have it off his chest. His dad was right about Abby. She was a survivor, willing to use anyone necessary to better her own situation. This family had weathered worse storms; they would weather this one too.

CHAPTER TWENTY TWO
BUILDING A NEW VICE

C huck Warner stood with a predatory glint in his eyes as he addressed the small assembly of his most trusted men in the dimly lit backroom of the trading post. The air hung thick with ambition and greed, magnified by his commanding presence.

"I want you to comb the town," Chuck instructed, his voice smooth like oil over steel. "Find the women who are desperate, the ones on the brink — those are the ones who need our protection."

The men, hardened by their allegiance to Chuck, nodded, understanding the unsavory undertones of the task at hand. They were well-versed in the art of manipulation and coercion, and the thought of preying on vulnerable women only seemed to embolden them further.

As Chuck's enforcers dispersed into the wounded

heart of the town, they prowled the streets and alleys with a hunter's focus. Their practiced eyes quickly identified several women whose poverty and strife painted them as perfect candidates for Chuck's offer of a safe haven.

The women, lured by the promise of steady work and security, found themselves being escorted back to the trading post. Eager faces lifted as they were introduced to Chuck, their new benefactor who pledged to care for them in exchange for their labor.

One of the group, Sarah, with her wary eyes and guarded stance, remained aloof. Something in Chuck's manner set off alarm bells in her head. She watched as the other women's faces lit up with hope, but she felt an icy trepidation gripping her heart.

That evening, Chuck and his men ensured their new 'recruits' were well-fed, encouraging them to enjoy the rare comfort of a hearty meal. The warm glow of the dining area saw the women relax for the first time in what felt like forever, with Sarah eyeing each joyous face skeptically.

Later, as the women were guided to the bathing area to wash away their past hardships, Chuck's true intentions began to seep through the facade. Behind a concealed viewing slot, Chuck and his inner circle silently appraised each woman, assigning them grades like prized livestock.

"Good start," Chuck murmured to his watchful compatriots, a twist of satisfaction in his gut. "But we're mostly sitting on 'C's with one 'B' in there."

They all nodded in agreement, dismissing the benevolence of this 'clean start' as merely a pretense for objectification. "We'll round up some more tomorrow," one of his men promised.

Chuck leaned back against the wall, thoughts churning. "There's an 'A' out at Cooper's place," he said, the words dripping with hunger. "A woman with fire in her veins. Make sure you bring her back, whatever it takes."

His men, eager to please their ruthless leader, assured him they would not fail. The seed of Chuck Warner's latest scheme was planted, and it would be nourished by exploitation and deceit.

Dawn broke with a chill in the air as three of Chuck's men approached the Cooper farm, their gait steady and determined, the subtle gleam of malice on their rugged faces. Each man bore a weapon that spoke of the business they intended to conduct — a business Chuck Warner himself had decreed.

Cooper, already up and working in the fields, noticed the approaching figures and lifted his tool in a wary greeting. His eyes narrowed as he recognized the men as working with Chuck Warner.

"We have a message from Chuck," the leader announced, a phony smile plastered across his face as they neared. "He's got some work for your wife, Terri. Says it's important."

Cooper's grip on his hoe tightened, his instincts flaring. "Terri won't be going anywhere with you," he spat resolutely, squaring his shoulders.

Anger crept into the leader's voice as he stepped forward. "Look, she can do this the easy way, or —"

But Cooper didn't let him finish. In one fluid motion, he retrieved a hidden shotgun from beside the barn and fired. The blast caught the leader full in the chest, sending him sprawling to the ground.

Chaos erupted. Guns drawn, the remaining two men unleashed a hail of bullets. Cooper, refusing to go down without a fight, returned fire but was struck down, a tragic casualty amidst the growing tension in the countryside.

Cooper laid motionless as the two men advanced, their victory short-lived when Terri emerged from the house, her own weapon drawn. The moment one stepped into her sights, she pulled the trigger, ending his life in a spray of blood and smoke.

The remaining man, furious and scared, ducked for cover and waited for his moment. Terri, knowing her husband's fate but driven by vengeance and the will to survive, scanned the horizon for the killer's position.

Their eyes met in a split second of acknowledgment before he charged, tackling Terri to the ground. The struggle was fierce; Terri fought like a wildcat, clawing and biting. But in the end, she was overpowered, her ferocity not enough against his brute strength.

Dragged away from the home she loved, Terri was hauled away under a sky still pink with the new dawn. The farm, once a haven of simple pleasures, now stood empty, a monument to the bloodshed that had occurred.

Within hours, Chuck received word of the events, displeasure flickering across his solemn features. "Bring her," he simply ordered upon hearing of Cooper's and his own men's demise.

And so, Terri, bound and bruised but unbroken in spirit, was brought before Chuck, tossed at his feet like a trophy. Their gazes locked — hers defiant, his coldly appraising.

"You're going to work for me now," Chuck declared, certain of his own invulnerability. Terri, her spirit a crescendo of loss and rage, vowed silently that no man, not even Chuck Warner, could truly claim her. She was already weaving plans of retribution as darkness settled in her heart, the sun a distant memory across a day stained with blood.

CHAPTER TWENTY THREE
A LOVELY NEW ARRIVAL

C huck Warner's lanky shadow fell over Terri, who sat bruised and bound on the hard wooden chair. Through the swelling and the grime, he could see her underlying resolve, the fiery defiance that flickered behind her eyes. He grinned; there was something thrilling in the prospect of bringing a woman like this under his control.

"Look at you," Chuck mused, the sibilant sound of his voice as chilling as the draft seeping through the floorboards. "You're stunning, even in this state. You'll be even more so after we've... familiarized you with our ways."

Terri's eyes blazed with suppressed rage, but her response was choked off by the gag she'd been forced to bite down on. Her skin crawled at Chuck's leering gaze, but she vowed not to give him the satisfaction of seeing her broken.

Chuck turned to his remaining man, who had just returned from disposing of the evidence of their skirmish at the Cooper farm. "See to it she's cleaned up and fed," he ordered, indifferent now to Terri's scathing silent seethe. "We want her looking her best for what's to come."

The man nodded, rough hands gripping Terri's arms as he hoisted her up and dragged her away into the depths of the trading post. Chuck watched them go with a smirk, anticipation coiling tight in his stomach.

Left alone in the room, Chuck settled back into his chair with an air of satisfaction. From his pocket, he pulled a small, battered notebook, filling out fresh pages with his swift, angular handwriting. Plans and people to see, the economy of Center Hill to further ensnare, families to manipulate — all mapped out with a strategist's precision.

His reverie, however, was broken by a peculiar sight. From the window, Chuck spied a flash of blonde pedaling determinedly towards the trading post. He rose, curiosity piqued, striding swiftly through the narrow corridors to greet this new opportunity.

As the blonde figure came closer, Chuck's

old instincts seized him. She was beautiful—an undeniable "A" in his twisted ranking system. The sight of her galvanized his senses. Fate, it seemed, had delivered yet another prize straight into his lap.

The girl dismounted with an unsteady grace, her large, innocent-looking eyes scanning the area until they settled on Chuck. She approached, her movements as graceful as a deer's, though far more daring. "Are you Chuck Warner?" she asked, the tone of her voice conveying a rare combination of vulnerability and boldness.

Chuck suppressed his surprise, responding with an easy smile. "I am, and who might you be, bringing such delightful beauty to my doorstep?"

"My name is Abby," her lips curled up sweetly, disarmingly. "And I think I have something that might interest you."

Chuck's smile widened further, a predator latching onto the words with a mixture of amusement and avarice. "Well, Abby," he said, closing the gap between them with the confidence of a man used to getting what he wanted. "I am all ears. Tell me, how might you assist me in expanding this thriving empire of mine?"

Abby leaned forward, eagerness glinting in her gaze as if she held the key to an unopened door and

Chuck, catching the gleam, was drawn inescapably to the prospect of unlocking it.

Chuck's curiosity was indeed piqued by this alluring visitor. What could this lovely girl possibly have to offer him, besides the obvious?

He invited Abby inside, ordering some food to be brought to them. As they ate, Abby turned on the charm, complimenting Chuck and appealing to his ego. "I've heard you're the most powerful man in these parts," she purred, fluttering her eyelashes. "A brilliant businessman and leader."

Chuck ate it up, utterly enamored by this manipulative vixen. She clearly knew how to stroke a man's ego.

As they dined on fine wine and food, Abby began divulging her true purpose. She told Chuck about Joe Kelly and his family, who were on their way to confront him.

Chuck seemed unconcerned, though a flicker of unease stirred within. He wasn't entirely prepared for another skirmish just yet.

"It's the same group who confronted you in New Leesburg," Abby added pointedly.

At this, Chuck's ears pricked up. His nonchalant facade momentarily slipped.

Then Abby delivered the real gut punch. She

told Chuck that his estranged wife Maria was with Joe's group...and in love with Joe.

Chuck struggled to contain his rage, though his face flushed red. How dare Maria betray their marriage vows, flee into the arms of this vagabond Joe Kelly!

But Chuck kept his turbulent emotions concealed. He continued conversing lightly with Abby, even as jealousy and vengeance churned within. This girl had delivered valuable intelligence indeed. Chuck would bide his time...then make them all pay.

Chuck gazed intently at Abby, his piercing eyes searching hers. "What is it you're looking for, Abby? Why are you here and not there with Joe Kelly's group?"

Abby dropped her coquettish act, her face growing serious. "I was with Joe's son, Jojo," she admitted. "But he rejected me for someone else." Bitterness tinged her words.

Chuck leaned back, a knowing smile playing on his lips. "Then the boy is a fool," he declared. "To let a beautiful, cunning woman like you get away? Utter stupidity."

Abby preened under the flattery, her lashes fluttering. "Jojo was just a boy. All impulse, no strategy. He didn't recognize my true talents." She sighed theatrically. "I need a real man. A man with power, who sees my potential."

She looked at Chuck through half-lidded eyes. "A man like you, Chuck. Jojo was nothing but a plaything. But you..." She traced a finger down his chest teasingly. "You could help me become so much more. With a strong, brilliant man like you by my side, we could build something great."

Chuck's eyes glinted with lustful pride. This girl knew exactly how to appeal to his desires - for power, for prestige, for possessing beauty. She would be an exquisite prize and a valuable ally.

"I see a hunger in you, Abby," Chuck purred. "A drive. You and I are far better suited than you ever were with that boy." He brushed a strand of golden hair from her face, his touch lingering. "Stay with me, and everything you ever dreamed will be yours. I'll teach you the art of strategy and empire building."

Abby's eyes shone with ambition. "I would love nothing more." She had cast her lot with this magnetic, dangerous man. And though unease flickered in her core, the lure of influence was far too tantalizing to resist.

CHAPTER TWENTY FOUR
INFILTRATION

Maria's pleading gaze fixed on Joe, her voice thick with urgency. "Please, Joe, let me come with you. I need to do this."

Joe shook his head, the lines on his face deepening. "It's too risky, Maria. You know that. If anyone there recognizes you—"

"But they won't," she interjected, the determination in her eyes belying her fear.

Joe placed his hands on her shoulders, a gesture meant to steady them both. "It's not a chance we can take. Your connection to Chuck—it's too dangerous."

A resigned sigh escaped Maria as she stepped back, her hands falling to her sides. Joe turned away, signaling the end of the discussion.

The group loaded up the van with supplies, each movement precise and practiced. Sam double-checked the ammo as Jake stowed away the first aid kit. Miguel ran a hand over his beard, eyes scanning the horizon before nodding at Claire who slipped into the passenger seat beside him.

They set out under a sky smeared with orange and purple hues, the van bouncing along dirt roads that hadn't seen maintenance in ages. The air grew tense as they neared Center Hill, each person lost in their own thoughts about what lay ahead.

Upon arrival at a secluded area outside Center Hill, they unloaded their gear and set up a makeshift base camp. Tents rose against the encroaching darkness; a fire crackled to life, its glow warding off the chill of the evening.

Once established, they split up, melting into the city like shadows at dusk. They threaded through abandoned streets and overgrown alleys with caution born from necessity.

Jojo adjusted his beret and made straight for the trading post, his stride confident but unassuming. The buzz of bartering voices grew louder as he approached—a cacophony of desperation and negotiation.

As he surveyed the crowd from beneath lowered brows, three men broke away from the throng and made a beeline for him. Jojo's instincts flared too late; rough hands grabbed him from behind.

He twisted violently, elbowing one in the ribs, but another man's fist found its mark against his temple. A burst of stars exploded across his vision before darkness swallowed him whole.

The darkness deepened as the night stretched on, each minute marked by the crackle of the fire and the hushed tones of the group. Joe paced the perimeter of their makeshift camp, his eyes scanning the road leading into town. His hands fidgeted with the zipper of his jacket, the repetitive motion belying his growing unease.

"He should've been back by now," Joe muttered, mostly to himself. The others exchanged uneasy looks.

"I'm sure he just got caught up, maybe found a good lead on supplies," Jake offered, though there was a note of doubt in his tone. Joe just shook his head, his jaw tight.

"Bones knows protocol. He wouldn't miss the rendezvous without reason." Sam's gravelly voice cut through the night air as he added another branch to the flames. Joe met his steady gaze and gave a curt nod. He could see the same concern etched on Sam's weathered features that Joe felt gnawing in his gut. Something wasn't right.

"We'll give it a few more minutes, but if he's not back soon, we need to go look for him," Joe said. Claire bit her lip, worry clouding her eyes. She looked to Miguel who stared pensively into the fire, the dancing flames reflected in his dark irises.

Joe resumed his pacing, dread filling his chest like rising floodwaters. His hands curled into fists as scenarios, each more troubling than the last, played through his mind. Finally, he came to a stop and turned to the others.

"Grab your gear. We're going back into town." His tone brooked no argument. As the group sprang into action, loading weapons and pulling on packs, Joe sent up a silent prayer that they would find Jojo in time. That nagging dread wouldn't subside until his son was safe again.

CHAPTER TWENTY FIVE
ABBY'S BETRAYAL

Jojo's head throbbed as he slowly regained consciousness. The last thing he remembered was standing in front of the trading post as three men approached him. Now he found himself in darkness, his wrists and ankles tightly bound. Panic rising in his chest, he yelled out, "Hello? Is anyone there?"

A metal door creaked open, letting in a sliver of light that pierced Jojo's eyes. A gruff voice said, "Well well, look who finally decided to wake up. The boss has been waiting to have a word with you."

Rough hands grabbed Jojo under the arms, hauling him to his feet. Still disoriented, Jojo squinted against the sunlight as he was dragged outside and around the back of the rundown trading post. That's when he saw him - Chuck Warner, arms crossed, an amused smile playing on his lips.

"Welcome back to the land of the living, Jojo," Chuck said. "Or do you prefer Junior? Joe Kelly's boy, isn't that right?"

Jojo's spine stiffened at the mention of his father's name. "How the hell do you know who I am?" he demanded. "What do you want, Warner?"

Chuck chuckled. "Let's just say a little birdie told me you'd be passing through. A beautiful, shapely blonde birdie."

Right on cue, the trading post door opened and out sauntered Abby, still as voluptuous as Jojo remembered. She gave him a sly smile. "Hey there, Jojo. Long time no see."

Jojo's shock quickly turned to anger. This was all Abby's doing. She had lured him into a trap, betraying him to the very man they all had come to despise. He strained against his bindings, rage boiling up inside of him. But Chuck and his men still held all the cards. All Jojo could do was glare at Abby's smug face, promising himself he'd make her regret this someday.

Jojo clenched his jaw as Abby sauntered over to Chuck, draping herself on his arm. "Did you miss me, baby?" she purred, looking up at Chuck adoringly.

Chuck gave her a patronizing pat on the head.

"That's enough, dear. The men are talking now."

Abby shot Jojo a venomous look before retreating inside the trading post.

Chuck turned his attention back to Jojo. "As I was saying, your father and I have some unfinished business. He took something important from me, and I aim to get it back."

Jojo's mind raced, wondering what his dad could have done to provoke the wrath of a dangerous man like Chuck Warner. But he wasn't about to give anything away.

"I don't know what you're talking about," Jojo said through gritted teeth. "And I sure as hell don't know where my old man is these days."

Chuck nodded thoughtfully. "I expected you'd say as much. No matter. You being here tells me Joe Kelly can't be far away. He'll come for you...and when he does, I'll be waiting."

He turned to his men. "Toss him back in the shed. We'll let him marinate for a while."

Rough hands grabbed Jojo again, shoving him back into the darkness. The door slammed shut, enveloping him in blackness once more. He slumped against the wall, heart pounding. His dad was walking right into a trap, and there was nothing Jojo could do to stop it.

Chuck strode back into the dingy trading post, the screen door banging shut behind him. Inside, Abby was perched on a stool at the counter, absently flipping through an old magazine. When she heard Chuck enter, she hopped up eagerly, sashaying over to him.

"Well, that was fun!" she exclaimed, draping herself against Chuck's broad chest. "Did you see the look on Jojo's face when he saw me? Priceless."

Chuck grabbed her arms roughly, shoving her away. "I thought I told you to keep your mouth shut unless I say otherwise," he growled.

Abby's face fell. She looked down, chastised. When she spoke again, her voice was quiet. "I'm sorry, I just got excited. But you wouldn't even know Joe and his people were in the area if it wasn't for me. I'm the one who told you Jojo would be coming through."

Chuck nodded begrudgingly. It was true, he owed this valuable piece of intelligence to Abby. She had a knack for wheedling information out of men, a skill that could prove useful.

"You're right," he conceded. "Just don't speak unless spoken to from now on. We have important business, and I can't have you running your mouth and messing things up. Understand?"

Abby was hurled against the wall by an unexpected and powerful grip on her throat. Her eyes bulged in terror as Chuck Warner towered over her, his gaze dark and unforgiving. For a moment, she thought he might kill her right here, right now. "You didn't listen to me, did you?" he growled, spittle flying from his lips. She shook her head frantically, trying to wriggle free. "I...I'm sorry, I just..." But those words caught in her throat, and she gulped for breath. Chuck guessed as much. He saw through her scheming, knew she was trying to manipulate him. How dare she! The stench of unwashed body and sweat washed over Abby as Chuck dragged her across the room. She felt rough hands forcing her against the wall, pushing aside a life-sized moose head that had been mounted for decoration. "I don't share," he grunted, spitting on the ground, his eyes ablaze with fury. Her clothes were yanked off in moments, leaving her exposed and shivering, despite the heat in the small room. Chuck was an animal, his hands rough and merciless as he threw her onto the dusty desk. It was a game to him. His nimble fingers unclenching her quivering body, priming her like she was one of his prey. Each thrust was harder than the last, and he groaned with satisfaction every time their flesh collided. Abby's pleas for him to stop fell on deaf ears, her body feeling like it was on fire. Her cries cut through the silence of the deserted trading post, muffled by Chuck's hand across her mouth.

Abby stared at her reflection in the grimy mirror of the trading post bathroom. Mascara smudged under her eyes, lipstick smeared across her cheek. She looked as broken on the outside as she felt within.

How could she have been so foolish, letting Chuck use her as his plaything? She thought she was smarter than that, better than that. But her arrogance had blinded her to the viper she'd aligned with.

She shuddered, the echoes of Chuck's violence still ringing in her ears. His hands around her throat, her desperate gasps for air. The snap of her bra strap as he tore her clothes away. The scrape of splintered floorboards against her back as he took her roughly, ignoring her cries of pain.

In the end, she was just a body to him. An object to be used and discarded for his pleasure. Not a woman, not even human. The realization sickened her.

Abby turned on the faucet, letting the water run hot. She scrubbed at her skin until it was raw, trying desperately to wash away Chuck's stench, his touch, his essence from her body. But she knew the scars ran deeper than skin. He had marked her, damaged her, shattered the illusion of control she once held over men.

She thought of Jojo then, bound and helpless in the shed behind the trading post. He must hate her now, and rightly so. She had served him up on a platter to the wolfish Chuck Warner, all because she thought it would gain her power. How foolish she had been. The only one with any power here was Chuck, and he wielded it like a brutal weapon.

Abby toweled off and dressed, avoiding the mirror now. She felt sick with herself, but more than that she felt afraid. Chuck was capable of anything - she knew that now more than ever. And he wouldn't let either her or Jojo leave here alive. Not when he was so close to getting his revenge on Joe Kelly.

She had to get to Jojo, convince him she wanted to help. It was the only way they might both escape Chuck's clutches. She only hoped Jojo would believe her, forgive her, though she knew she didn't deserve his trust. Not after what she'd done.

CHAPTER TWENTY SIX
TENSION AT TWILIGHT

B ack at the cabin, Maria paced the floor like a caged animal, her worry etching deep grooves in the worn wooden planks. Every creak of the boards, every whisper of wind through the cracks, seemed to echo her inner turmoil. Joe was out there, in Chuck Warner's dangerous world, and her mind reeled with the possibilities that he might not return.

Taylor watched Maria's restless motion, her own heart a cauldron of concern. With her little one, Parker, nestled against her shoulder, she spoke in hushed, soothing tones, "Maria, dad knows what he's doing. He's careful and smart. He'll come back to us, you'll see."

Toni, seated by the fireplace, chimed in, her voice steady despite the undercurrent of her own fears. "My son's survived worse than that weasel

Chuck Warner. If there's one thing I've learned, it's that Joe's got more lives than a cat."

But despite her words, Toni's fingers knotted and twisted the hem of her skirt, her gaze distant and clouded with the possibility of never seeing Joe or Jojo again.

Taylor swayed gently, the rhythmic motion lulling Parker into a peaceful state, an innocent contrast to the tension filling the room. Her heart ached not just for her father and brother, but for Jake, her steadfast rock. Every second dragged by like an eternity, each tick of the old wall clock a reminder of the silence that stretched between the cabin and the unknown fate of her family.

Maria turned to her friends, each gripped in their own private hells, and tried to draw strength from their presence. The connection they shared, knitted from shared fear and hope, was the only thing keeping the gnawing dread at bay.

Paulette stepped into the cabin, the door creaking open to reveal the anxious faces of Maria, Taylor, and Toni. Beside her stood a teenage girl, thin and tentative, her eyes darting around the room.

Sensing the palpable tension hanging in the air, Paulette forced a smile. "Hey there, no need to be afraid. I know Joe Kelly and he won't let anything bad happen." She tried to make her voice bright and reassuring. "C'mon girls, there's no need for worry here."

The words sounded hollow even to her own ears. In her mind, Paulette couldn't escape her own gnawing fears for her son, Jojo. She hadn't seen him in years. Now he was out there, in harm's way, and the possibility that she might never get to make things right gripped her heart like a vise.

Paulette steadied herself with a deep breath, pushing the dark thoughts away. She focused on the young girl at her side, this scrap of humanity she'd found alone and trembling after days without food or shelter. At least here, surrounded by the warmth of the fire and the company of others, this child could find some small comfort amidst the surrounding chaos. Paulette gently squeezed the girl's shoulder, a silent promise that she would not leave her to face the darkness alone.

As the stars began to dot the evening sky, the women gathered closer, their mutual fear unspoken but palpable in the room. Maria, Taylor, Toni and Paulette held onto each other, each woman silently praying for the safe return of Joe and the men who had left the safety of the cabin to face Chuck Warner head-on.

CHAPTER TWENTY SEVEN
SEARCH AND REGRETS

The early morning air was crisp, carrying the earthy scent of the forest as Joe led the group away from their makeshift base camp. Sam checked his watch, a habit from old times, though it no longer measured their days or nights. Claire hoisted her pack, the weight familiar and oddly comforting on her back, while Miguel and Jake surveyed the treeline, alert to every rustle, every shift in the quiet woodland chorus.

As they neared the town, the comforting canopy of trees gave way to the scarred landscape left in the wake of recent turmoil. Buildings, once signs of a thriving community, now stood as hollowed remains—a testament to the fragility of order.

"Our first stop is the trading post," Joe said, his voice low but filled with a steely determination. "If Chuck's got Jojo, that's where he'll be."

Miguel nodded in agreement, his hand resting casually near the hilt of his knife. Jake swept the town with his watchful gaze, his own resolve mirroring Joe's. Sam cracked his knuckles, a subconscious echo of readiness. Claire glanced at each of her companions in turn, her own apprehension buried beneath a hardened exterior.

The group moved with purpose, a silent understanding flowing between them. Their eyes rarely lingered on the desolation surrounding them; there was only the mission and the narrow hope that Jojo still lived. They skirted abandoned cars and debris-strewn streets like specters, the echo of their steps a haunting rhythm in the quiet town.

As they approached the trading post, the signs of Chuck Warner's influence were everywhere — from the wary glances of the downtrodden townsfolk to the heavy-footed guards stationed around the perimeter. They were careful to stay out of sight, using the shell of a collapsed storefront for cover.

Joe peered around the jagged edge of brick and mortar, his eyes locked on the trading post's door — the dilapidated building that now served as a throne room for a tyrant. His mouth drew into a line and when he spoke, his voice was barely a whisper.

"There," he pointed, "keep your heads down

and follow my lead."

One by one, they advanced, their shadows stretching long and thin in the early morning light, a subtle portent of the confrontation to come.

Joe crouched low behind the rusting shell of an abandoned pickup truck, its faded red paint barely visible beneath years of dirt and decay. Across the street, he could see Sam hunkering down behind the crumbling wall of a building, his face etched with grim determination. Jake and Miguel had taken up positions on adjacent streets surrounding the trading post, while Claire was stationed on the rooftop of a small grocery store overlooking the entire scene.

Joe's heart pounded as his mind raced with possibilities, each more horrific than the last. Was his son even still alive? And if he was, what tortures had Chuck Warner inflicted upon him? Joe clenched his jaw, rage and anguish churning inside him like a storm. He had to maintain control. He couldn't let his emotions get the better of him, not when Jojo's life hung in the balance.

Taking a deep breath, Joe steadied his nerves and focused his attention on the trading post. The guards standing at attention outside were heavily armed, assault rifles held casually in their hands as if they were simply out for a leisurely stroll. Joe's eyes narrowed as he studied their patterns of movement, looking for any weakness, any opportunity to gain entry undetected.

Meanwhile, Claire watched the scene unfolding below her, perched like a sentinel from her rooftop vantage point. Her long blonde hair was pulled back tightly and her eyes, usually so vibrant, were now hard and dark, mirroring the dread in her heart. Visions of Jojo, battered and broken, flashed through her mind, and she had to choke back a sob. She had vowed not to reveal their secret relationship to the others until Jojo was safe, but now she questioned that decision. If he didn't make it out alive, the regret would haunt her forever.

Steeling herself, she pushed aside those thoughts. Jojo was a fighter, a survivor. She had to believe he was still holding on somehow. Gripping her rifle tightly, she swore that if they succeeded in rescuing him, she would shout her love for him from the rooftops. No more hiding, no more secrets. If they survived this, everyone would know.

CHAPTER TWENTY EIGHT
DESPERATE DAMSELS

C huck Warner sat behind the large desk in his corner office overlooking the trading post. Though it was nearly sunset, he hadn't turned on any lights, preferring the dark shadows and the illusion of privacy they provided. He called for Karl, one of his most trusted men.

"Bring me Terri and Sarah," he instructed in his usual brisk tone. Karl didn't need any further explanation. He knew exactly why Chuck had summoned the two women. Of all the people living under Chuck's control in the trading post, Terri and Sarah remained the most defiant, constantly testing the boundaries and refusing to bend to Chuck's will. He would need to make an example of them, to train them into proper submission through whatever means necessary. It was regrettable but required. Chuck had grand plans for this place, and he needed total obedience to realize his vision.

Chuck settled back in his leather chair, steepled his fingers and waited. Before long, a sharp rap at the door announced Karl's return. "Come in," Chuck commanded. The door swung open and Karl entered, forcibly dragging the two women with him. Terri struggled against Karl's grip on her arm, while Sarah remained unsettlingly still, her face an emotionless mask. Chuck nodded in approval at Karl's handling of the situation. "You may go," he dismissed the man, who gratefully left, pulling the heavy door closed behind him.

Now alone with his two captives, Chuck rose from his desk and circled the women slowly, hands clasped behind his back. He could sense their fear and defiance rolling off of them in waves. Good, he thought. It will make things easier.

"Ladies," he began smoothly. "I think we need to have a little talk about obedience..."

Sarah's jaw clenched, her hands balling into fists at her sides. Terri let out a strangled sob, tears spilling down her cheeks.

Chuck paused in front of them, his eyes cold and calculating. "I have a client arriving later who is in need of some...let's just call it companionship," he said, his voice dripping with sinister implication.

"Now, I am not particular about which one of you provides that service."

He checked the expensive watch on his wrist. "You have one minute to decide. If one of you volunteers, the other will be spared...for now. If neither of you steps forward, you will both service my client."

Terri's sobs grew louder, her body trembling. Sarah remained motionless, her expression stony.

Chuck began counting down from sixty, each number pronounced with chilling nonchalance. "Fifty-nine...fifty-eight..."

Terri fell to her knees, grasping at the hem of Sarah's shirt. "Sarah, please!" she begged between sobs. "I can't do this!"

Sarah kept her eyes fixed straight ahead, giving no indication she had even heard.

"Thirty...twenty-nine..." Chuck continued counting down.

With a broken wail, Terri buried her face in her hands. Sarah closed her eyes, a single tear escaping down her cheek.

The last number was uttered. Chuck smiled coldly. "I guess you've both made your choice then." He strode to the door and held it open. "Come. My client will be here in a while, you two need to prepare."

Chuck ushered Sarah and Terri down the dim hallway, his hand firmly gripping each of their arms. He led them to a nondescript door and opened it, shoving them inside the small room.

"Wait here," he commanded. "My client will be joining you in a bit." With that, he pulled the door closed and locked it from the outside.

The two women stood frozen, clinging to each other for what seemed an eternity. Eventually they heard the sounds of muffled footsteps approaching. Suddenly the door swung open and a large, elderly man lumbered into the room. His lips curled into a lecherous grin as he saw the two young women awaiting him.

"Well, well, what do we have here?" he rasped excitedly. "Two lovely ladies just for me? Old Chuck sure knows how to treat a guest."

He rubbed his hands together greedily. "Alright my dears, let's get this party started. Slowly take off those clothes for me."

Sarah and Terri exchanged a frightened look, then slowly began removing their shirts and pants, tears streaming down their cheeks.

The man's eyes devoured their nearly naked bodies hungrily. "Come here, darling," he crooned at Sarah, beckoning her closer with a gnarled finger.

Sarah shuddered but did as she was told, stepping toward him. As she did, Terri noticed an iron sitting on a small table across the room. Keeping her eyes downcast, she moved around the other side of the bed, closer to the potential weapon.

"On the bed, both of you," the man commanded. Sarah perched nervously on the edge of the mattress. As the man slid closer to her, Terri grabbed the iron and hefted it over her shoulder.

Just as the man wrapped his arms around Sarah, Terri swung with all her might, connecting the iron to the back of his head with a sickening crack.

Sarah stood frozen, staring down at the man's twitching body as blood pooled beneath his head. The iron slipped from Terri's fingers, clattering to the floor.

"Oh my god," Terri whispered, her voice quivering. "I...I think I killed him."

Sarah remained silent, slowly turning her gaze to meet Terri's terrified eyes. After a long moment, she knelt and pressed her fingers to the man's neck, feeling for a pulse. Nothing.

"He's dead," she confirmed flatly, rising back to her feet.

Terri let out a strangled sob, her hands flying

to cover her mouth. Sarah grabbed her shoulders firmly.

"Listen to me," she urged. "We need to move, now. Get dressed."

Sarah snatched up their discarded clothes and shoved Terri's shirt and pants at her. The two women scrambled to redress with shaking hands. Sarah kept stealing glances at the door, expecting Chuck or one of his men to come bursting in at any moment.

Once dressed, Sarah hurried to the room's only window and shoved it open. It was small and high up the wall, but it would have to do. She peered out - they were on the second floor, but there was a drainage pipe running down the brick exterior close enough to grab onto.

"Come on," Sarah said, gesturing to Terri. Together they hoisted themselves up and out the window, gripping the metal pipe tightly. Sarah went first, nimbly making her way down using both her hands and feet. Terri followed more slowly, nearly slipping once in her panicked state.

Finally they reached the ground. The trading post was eerily quiet, most people long asleep in their bunks at this late hour, but the sun would be rising soon, they needed to move quickly. Keeping to the shadows, Sarah and Terri crept toward the perimeter fence. A patrolling guard walked by and they pressed themselves flat against the side of a building, holding their breath. Once he had passed, they sprinted the last stretch of open ground to the fence. Sarah gave Terri a leg up and over the chain link barrier, then clambered over herself.

And then they were free, disappearing into the woods beyond the fences of Chuck Warner's domain. Adrenaline pumped through Sarah's veins as they ran, branches whipping against their skin. But it was a small price to pay for escape. She didn't know where they would go or how long they could evade Chuck's grasp, but at least for now, they had won their freedom.

* * * * * * * * * * * * * * * * * * *

The woods were dense with shadow as Sarah and Terri crashed through the underbrush, their breaths coming in panicked gasps. Thorns tore at their clothes and skin, but they barely felt the stings, focused only on putting as much distance between themselves and their pursuers as possible.

Suddenly, a large figure stepped out from behind a tree directly in their path. Sarah yelped in surprise and Terri let out a shriek, both skidding to a halt in front of the imposing man. He was unshaven, with a jagged scar cutting across his cheek and a flinty look in his deep brown eyes. The women froze like deer in headlights, unsure whether to bolt or plead for mercy.

"Easy now, I'm not going to hurt you," the man said, holding up his hands. His voice was gruff but even. "Name's Miguel. You're safe here."

Terri's eyes welled up with tears of relief, but Sarah remained wary. Before Miguel could react, she leapt at him in a blur, knocking him back a step as she clawed at his face.

"No!" a female voice shouted. A young blonde woman sprinted from the trees, followed closely by a lean, uniformed man and an older guy with salt-and-pepper hair. Together they pulled Sarah off Miguel, who stood unfazed with only a few light scratches from her nails.

"Settle down, we're here to help," the older man said in a gentle tone as the blonde went to comfort a sobbing Terri. Miguel rubbed his cheek absently, his expression remaining neutral.

Sarah trembled, the fight draining out of her as the reality of their situation sunk in. "He...Chuck...he was going to force us into prostitution for his stupid trading post!" she sputtered, her words spilling out in a rush. "Said we owed him for taking us in. But we didn't want to, we just wanted somewhere safe to stay, but he...." Her voice broke and she buried her face in her hands.

The group exchanged dark looks, anger simmering in their eyes. "Chuck Warner's nothing but a parasite looking to profit off this disaster," the older man practically spat. "And now he's taken my boy. My son -

Sarah lifted her head from her hands, wiping the tears from her eyes. "Your son...what did he look like?" she asked Joe hesitantly.

Joe's expression softened slightly. "He's a tall young man, muscular build. Keeps his hair in a military-style cut. Never seen without his tan beret - it was part of his old Army uniform."

Hope flashed across Sarah's face. "I saw him! Yesterday, Chuck's men brought him in. They hit him from behind." Her face fell. "They beat him pretty bad to get him under control. I saw them throw him in that shed out behind the trading post."

Joe paled, his hands clenching into fists. "Is he still there?" he asked urgently. "Did you see him today?"

Sarah nodded quickly. "As far as I know. Chuck's

planning to..." She trailed off, a look of anguish on her face.

Joe's jaw tightened, fury smoldering in his eyes. He turned to Sam. "Get everyone ready. We've got to get to that shed." Sam nodded curtly, his expression grim. Joe turned back to Sarah, his voice gentler. "What can you tell us about the layout of the place, can we get to that shed without alerting the guards?

Sarah took a shaky breath, then began describing what she'd seen of Chuck's heavily fortified operation. Joe and the others listened intently, already forming a plan. One way or another, Joe would free his son from that madman's clutches. Chuck had no idea the hell that was about to rain down on him.

* * * * * * * * * * * * * * * * * * * *

Joe turned to Sam, his face etched with grim determination. "We need to assess the situation. How many guards are we dealing with? What are their rotations? Is there enough cover for us to get in unseen?"

Sam nodded, scanning the ramshackle trading post with a tactician's eye. "We've got to get eyes on that shed first. See their security setup, find any weaknesses we can exploit."

Joe clasped Sam's shoulder firmly. Then he turned to Sarah and Terri, "Listen, I've got a safe place for you both set up on the outskirts of town. It's our base camp for now. Head there and wait for us. We'll come get you as soon as we have my boy back, then take you somewhere secure."

Sarah's eyes welled with grateful tears. "Oh Joe, thank you. I wasn't sure we'd make it until you found us."

"You saved our lives," added Terri. "We'll do whatever you say."

Joe squeezed their hands supportively. "You'll be safe at the camp. My family and I need to handle this, but we'll be back for you soon."

The two women gathered their courage and slipped away, following the directions Joe had given them. Joe turned to the others, his jaw set. "Let's go get my son back."

Claire, Miguel, and Jake nodded, faces steeled with resolve. Together, they crept through the woods bordering the ramshackle trading post until they had a vantage point of the shed. Jake peered through binoculars, surveying the layout.

"There's a guard stationed at each corner of

the shed. Two more patrolling the grounds on an irregular sweep pattern. I don't see any snipers or surveillance advantage points they could use against us," he reported.

"Windows are boarded up, just the one entrance," added Claire, hunkered down beside him. "We can use those rusted out trucks for cover getting closer."

Joe listened intently, tactical gears churning. "Let's move under that ridge, use the overgrowth as cover. I'll take the first guard, then Claire, you and Miguel take the one to the east. Jake and Sam, the other two are yours. We hit them fast and quiet. Once we have Jojo, we exfiltrate back into the woods."

The group moved wordlessly into position. Suddenly a figure emerged from the trading post and headed towards the shed. This was an unexpected new wrinkle in the plan. They watched from each of their vantage points not knowing quite what to do next but still waiting on a signal from Joe. The figure was that of a female and she seemed familiar. There was no doubt, it was Abby.

Joe stunned at Abby's presence here, waited and held his signal to see how this played out. The reality of her betrayal hit him like a ton of bricks.

Abby sauntered up to one the guards and said,

"Chuck wanted me to get some more information from him, if you know what I mean." The guard looked her up and down approvingly, "Well he certainly sent the right person, I'd tell you anything baby." Abby rolled her eyes, "Just open the damn door Romeo and let me do my thing."

The guard hesitated for a moment fumbling for his keys, "All right, All right keep your panties on honey, or maybe not as the case may be." He laughed.

As Abby entered the shed the guard shut the door behind her and motioned for the other three guards to come around to the front. As they did, he told them to listen carefully, they were about to get a show.

Joe, Claire, Sam, Miguel and Jake slowly started making their way closer to the back of the shed now that all the guards were huddled in the front.

Once inside Abby made a beeline for Jojo and began cutting his restraints. Groggy and weakened Jojo looked up at her, "What are you…." Abby put a finger to her lips. "We've got to get you out of here, Chuck is evil and he'll kill you once he gets what he wants. I snuck this knife, there are four guards out there around the shed. Are you strong enough to move?"

Just then a heavy thud sounded at the front door along with the sounds of scuffling and muffled voices. Abby's eyes filled with terror as the door swung open. Standing in the doorframe was Joe. Relief flooded through him at the sight of Jojo's familiar frame. His boy was alive. They were getting him back.

He turned his gun towards Abby's head, "You treacherous little bitch." Jojo grabbed Abby and pulled her towards him, "Dad NO, she just came in to rescue me. Put the gun down."

As Joe lowered his gun Claire appeared in the doorway seeing Jojo holding Abby close in his arms.

* * * * * * * * * * * * * * * * * * *

Jojo noticed Claire's eyes starting to tear as she stood in the doorway, her chest heaving with each breath. She turned to his father and said with urgency in her voice, "We need to move out of here. Now."

Joe didn't hesitate. He moved swiftly to help Jojo to his feet, throwing Jojo's arm around his shoulders to support his weight. "You heard her boys, let's move," he commanded.

Working quickly and efficiently, they dragged

the four guards' lifeless bodies into the dilapidated shed, leaving them in a heap on the dirt floor. With the evidence of their skirmish now hidden, it was time to move out. Abby still on the ground with her face in her hands started to cry. The group turned and looked at one another. Joe looking to Jojo, "You're call son." As Jojo began to stammer Claire interrupted, "Bring her, if nothing else she's got intel on this place." Sam reached down and helped Abby to her feet. They all slipped out and moved swiftly towards the treeline about twenty yards away.

They moved as swiftly as they could through the dense forest, but Jojo's injuries slowed their pace. With every labored breath, he winced from the stabbing pain in his ribs. Claire noticed him struggling and wordlessly offered her shoulder for support. He managed a pained smile in thanks as they continued on.

After two hours of steady movement, Joe called for a break. Jojo gingerly lowered himself onto a fallen log, sweat beading on his forehead. Claire crouched next to him, gently probing his torso to assess the damage. "Nothing feels broken, but you should take it easy," she said softly.

From across the makeshift camp, Abby tentatively approached Claire. "I just wanted to say thank you again for convincing them to bring me along," she said. "I know how much you all must hate me after everything I've done."

Claire's eyes flashed with anger. "Who said I forgave you?" she asked sharply. "You deliberately tried to come between me and Jojo. You used him and you used me. I vouched for you because leaving you there wasn't an option, not because I've forgotten who you are."

Abby looked down, ashamed. "You're right," she said quietly. "I heard you two talking about having feelings for each other and I was jealous. I wanted Jojo for myself and I didn't care who I hurt. I know now how selfish I was. I promise I'll never come between you two again. I want to change, to be a better person, if you'll let me."

Claire studied her for a long moment, then gave a curt nod. "Prove it then. We've got a long road ahead." She stood abruptly and returned to Jojo's side, leaving Abby to ponder her words.

Sarah breathed a sigh of relief as Joe and the others emerged from the tree line into the clearing where the basecamp was located. She had been pacing anxiously, waiting for any sign of their return. When she saw Joe supporting a battered Jojo, with Sam and Claire close behind carrying supplies, she rushed over.

"Thank God you made it!" she exclaimed, embracing Joe tightly. "And it looks like you got your son back too."

Joe returned the hug briefly before pulling back, his expression serious. "Yeah we were lucky this time," he said grimly. "But we've got to get out of here and back home before that luck runs out."

He turned and shouted to the rest of the group milling about the camp. "Alright everyone, listen up! I want us packed up and on the road in the next fifteen minutes. Get the van loaded up, we're getting out of here now."

Everyone sprang into action, dismantling tents and packing gear with efficient haste. Sam and Terri supported Jojo over to the van and helped ease him into the back seat. Claire grabbed medical supplies to tend to his injuries on the road. Abby lingered on the edge of the camp, looking unsure where to help until Jake directed her to assist with taking down one of the tents.

Within ten minutes, the camp was fully dismantled and the group was crammed into the van. Joe jumped into the driver's seat, cranked the ignition, and peeled out down the dirt road away from the basecamp. As the compound faded into the distance behind them, a collective sense of relief spread through the van. They had survived one close call, but who knew what lay ahead on the long road home. For now, they took comfort in each other's company as the van rumbled down the deserted backroads. There would be time to plan their next move, but first, they needed to put some distance between themselves and this place. Joe's knuckles were white on the steering wheel, his jaw set with determination. After everything, he would stop at nothing to get his family home safely.

Joe gripped the steering wheel tighter, his knuckles turning white. The van was silent except for the rumble of the tires on the cracked asphalt. No one spoke a word, each passenger lost in their own thoughts about the day's harrowing events.

After several long minutes, Abby tentatively broke the silence. "Everyone, I want to apologize for what I've done," she began haltingly. "I've been selfish and reckless." She took a deep breath before continuing. "I can't ask for your forgiveness, but I promise I'm a changed woman after seeing the pure evil that is Chuck Warner and all the other evil out there in this new world we're living in. I promise to do everything I can to make amends."

Joe's eyes flicked up to meet Abby's in the

rearview mirror. "I hope you're serious about that, Abby," he said gruffly. "At least you're safe now and we got Jojo back, so no real harm came of it in the end."

Abby held his gaze, her expression pained. "Well, there is more I need to tell you," she said hesitantly.

Joe's eyes narrowed. "And what's that?" he asked sharply.

Abby looked down at her hands, unable to meet his piercing stare. "I told Chuck about you and your family and where you are and...and...about Maria being with you," she confessed in a rush.

Joe's grip on the wheel was now bone-white. The van swerved slightly before he regained control. "You did what?" he asked in a low, dangerous tone.

"I'm so sorry," Abby said desperately. "He manipulated me, made me think he actually cared about me. I know now it was all lies. But at the time, I told him everything - where your cabin is, who is with you, about Maria and your...relationship."

Joe was breathing heavily, his jaw clenched. The others in the van looked on in shocked silence.

"Do you have any idea what you've done?" Joe ground out. "The danger you've put us all in? My family?"

"I know, and I'm so sorry," Abby said, her voice breaking. "At the time, I thought I was doing the right thing, that Chuck could provide safety and security. I know now how wrong I was. I'll do anything to make this right, anything at all."

Joe was silent, staring straight ahead at the road, his hands clenched white on the wheel. The van filled with tense silence once more.

Finally, Joe spoke. "It's too late for sorry," he said coldly. "The damage is already done. Now we have to figure out how to survive what's coming next, no thanks to you."

Abby dropped her head in shame, tears filling her eyes. The others exchanged uneasy glances, realizing the full implications of what she had revealed. Their location was compromised, and Chuck Warner was coming for them, with unknown forces at his disposal. Joe stared straight ahead into the growing darkness, his mind racing through their limited options. After a long, fraught silence, he made a decision.

"We're not going back to the cabin," he announced. "That life is over thanks to Abby here. We need a new plan." He met Jojo's eyes in the rearview mirror, a silent question passing between them. Jojo gave a subtle nod of agreement. A new course was set, into an uncertain future. But come what may, Joe would protect his family - no matter the cost.

* * * * * * * * * * * * * * * * * * *

Joe pulled the van up to the cabin, his jaw clenched tight. Abby had spilled their location to Chuck Warner, putting them all in danger. He killed the engine and sat there a moment, rubbing his calloused hands over his weathered face.

"Dammit," he muttered under his breath. He'd been a fool to let Abby stick around as long as he did, but he couldn't change the past. All he could do now was get his family someplace safe, and fast.

Stepping out of the van, he strode into the cabin. "Pack your things," he announced gruffly. "We're movin' out of here as soon as we can."

Taylor looked up. "What's going on, Dad?"

Joe's lips pressed into a thin line. "Abby told Chuck where we're holed up. We gotta get to a more secure location before they come for us, and they will come for us eventually."

The color drained from Taylor's face where she sat feeding Parker. "Oh god. What are we going to do?"

"What we should've done long ago," Joe said. "Find a place we can fortify and defend."

He turned to Jojo and Miguel. "I want you two suited up and ready to ride along with me and Jake first thing tomorrow. We'll go out and scout a location, someplace easy to secure where we can build a life."

Miguel nodded. "I'm with you."

Joe clapped him on the shoulder. "Good man."

They spent the rest of the evening preparing for the big move, gathering weapons and critical supplies. At dawn, Joe, Jojo, Miguel, Jake and Sam piled into Joe's van and headed out in search of their new home.

After miles of backroads and abandoned properties, they came across an old factory warehouse surrounded by a chain link fence topped with coils of razor wire.

"Well, would you look at that," Joe said, a grin spreading across his weathered face. This was perfect - already fortified, plenty of space, even had its own well system. A little TLC and this place would be an ideal homestead.

The others nodded in agreement as they explored the grounds. This would do nicely. They could build a real life here, a safe haven for their family.

Energized by the prospect, they hurried back to gather up the rest of the group. Over the next few days, they began the arduous but satisfying work of transporting their supplies to the new location, back and forth, throughout each day and throughout each night.

By week's end, they had successfully relocated everyone and were ready to begin transforming the old warehouse into a secure home. As he gazed around at the vast space that was now theirs, Joe felt a swell of hope. This could work. They could make this work. Finally, they had a real shot at building a future.

Joe called everyone together for a meeting in the large open area of the warehouse. As the group of 47 gathered around, Joe stepped forward to address them.

"We've got a growing number of people here now, last count puts us at forty seven," Joe began. "And while we've got some supplies, it's not nearly enough to sustain us long term."

Murmurs rippled through the crowd as they nodded solemnly.

"So we need to get organized, now more than ever," Joe continued. "There's a few essential things we need to survive - food, water, shelter, and defense. I'm suggesting we organize ourselves into committees and subcommittees for each of these needs."

Joe scanned the room. "I need volunteers for each of these committees. The food committee will be responsible for getting us food - that means scavenging what's left out there, hunting, gardening, and whatever else you can think of."

Taylor and several other women raised their hands, volunteering to start gardening with the seeds Joe had stored away. Joe's mother, Toni, also raised her hand. "I'm an expert at canning. I can lead the preservation of any food we bring in."

Joe nodded. "Great. What about water? We need to not only find sources, but look at catching rainwater and storage."

Several others volunteered for the water committee.

"Excellent," Joe said. "Now shelter - we've got a good start here, but we need people to keep making improvements every day."

More hands went up for the shelter committee.

"And finally, defense." Joe's expression turned grim. "This committee will work hand in hand with the shelter group, but I also want a plan to ambush Chuck and his men when they eventually come.

If we plan this right, we might just be able to take Chuck out for good."

The crowd murmured, a mix of anxiety and resolve on their faces.

"I'll select the defense committee myself," Joe said. "It'll be myself, Jojo, Jake, Miguel, Sam, and Claire. We'll come up with plans to defend this place and lay a trap for Chuck."

Joe scanned the room one last time. "Are we all agreed?"

"YES!" the crowd yelled back, a new energy and excitement among them.

"Right then, let's get to work," Joe said. "Each group, break out and start your plans. We need to move fast."

With that, the meeting broke up into smaller groups, ready to take on their new roles and start building their survival stronghold.

Joe nodded with satisfaction as the groups dispersed to begin their planning. This was exactly what they needed - everyone working together towards a common goal. With Chuck still out there biding his time, they had to be ready.

Jojo gathered the defense committee together. "Alright, here's the situation. We got the advantage of this location being unknown to Chuck. We need to use that to set a trap, take him and his men by surprise."

Claire crossed her arms. "What did you have in mind?"

"Some kind of decoy to lure them in. Then when they least expect it, we hit them from all sides."

Miguel rubbed his chin thoughtfully. "Could work. We rig explosives on the road leading here. When they drive over it..." He mimed an explosion with his hands.

Sam grinned. "I like the way you think, brother."

Jojo started pacing as he thought it through. "We set charges along the road, use the woods for cover. As soon as the vehicles pass, we detonate. Then come in hard and fast from the tree lines to finish them off."

Joe listened intently, leaning against the wall with his arms crossed. "Solid plan. But we need to lure them there first. Make 'em think we're still back at the cabin."

"A decoy team," Jake suggested. "Make it seem like we're still there, keep them distracted."

Taylor looked uneasy. "I don't know, it's pretty risky."

Joe put a hand on her shoulder. "Don't you worry, we'll keep the decoy team small. And they won't engage, just get Chuck's attention. In and out."

She sighed. "Alright Dad, I trust you."

"That's my girl." He turned to Claire. "You'll lead the decoy team, draw them off our trail. Take Miguel and one other, your choice."

Claire nodded firmly, determined. "Consider it done."

The team hashed out the specifics - timing, positioning, coordinating the detonation. The plan was to lure Chuck's forces in to a certain point and then detonate explosives at the rear of his forces, trapping the forces in front of them, and then picking them off with more explosives and sniper fire from the treeline. After an hour of discussion, they had a solid plan of attack.

Joe clapped his hands together. "Okay people, let's get to work. We don't have much time."

With newfound purpose, the defense committee headed out to begin preparations. Rigging explosives, stockpiling ammo, planning their positions down to the last detail. This was it - their chance to finally take the fight to Chuck. Failure was not an option. It was time to end this threat once and for all. All they needed to do now was plan, prepare and wait.

CHAPTER TWENTY NINE
REALIZATION AND REVENGE

C huck surveyed the area around the shed behind the trading post, his rage boiling inside at the scene before him. Four of his best men lay dead on the dusty floor, their throats slit ear to ear. This was the work of Joe Kelly, he was certain. The old fool had somehow managed to free his son Jojo from right under Chuck's nose.

Chuck spat on the ground in disgust. He had just come from the upstairs room of the trading post where his most profitable client lay motionless on the bed, his head crushed from an iron that lay next to him. The man's pants were down around his ankles, his desires left unfulfilled. Chuck's girls, Sarah and Terri, were nowhere to be found. Like rats deserting a sinking ship.

Chuck barked out, "Victor! Get over here now!"

Seconds later, Victor came jogging up, slightly

out of breath. "Yeah boss?"

Chuck gestured angrily at the carnage. "You see what that old goat Kelly did? He snuck in here and took out my men, freed his son, and killed my best client. And now my girls have disappeared too."

Victor nodded slowly, his expression grim. "So what do you want to do about it?"

Chuck gripped Victor's shoulder firmly, his fingers digging in. "What do you think? I want you to take some men and hunt Kelly down. Bring me back that treacherous wife of mine while you're at it. She's with them according to that slutty little blonde, who by the way is missing as well."

Victor hesitated. "I'm not sure we have the manpower right now to launch an attack boss. We lost some guys last week in that skirmish at the fuel depot. Maybe I should take some time, get our numbers back up before going after Kelly and his crew."

Chuck's eyes blazed with fury. "I want revenge and I want it now! Not next week! You get off your ass and make this happen or I'll find someone who can."

Sweat beaded Victor's forehead. "Okay, okay," he stammered. "Just give me a few days to put a plan together and rally more men. I'll get it done, don't worry."

Chuck jabbed his finger into Victor's chest. "You have one week, no more. And you damn well better not fail me."

Victor swallowed hard. "I won't let you down boss, I promise."

Chuck scowled. "For your sake, you better not." He turned and stalked away, leaving Victor standing there, already dreading the task ahead. One week was not nearly enough time, but he knew better than to argue. When Chuck wanted revenge, he would stop at nothing to get it. Victor could only hope he could deliver the results Chuck demanded before that murderous rage was turned on him instead.

Victor walked over to his top lieutenant Noah, who was leaning against the trading post wall smoking a cigarette.

"We've got a problem," Victor said grimly. Noah flicked his cigarette to the ground. "Yeah, I see that. What the hell happened here?"

Victor shook his head. "Kelly and his boy somehow got the jump on Chuck's guards. Freed the kid and took off. Chuck's furious, wants revenge on Kelly now."

Noah let out a low whistle. "Revenge, huh?

Guess Chuck's got a death wish for us all."

Victor nodded. "He wants us to hit Kelly's compound, bring back his wife. Says we've got a week."

"A week?" Noah scoffed. "We just got torn up bad on that fuel run. I'd say we're down to maybe sixty, seventy able bodies tops."

"That's what I figured," Victor said. "We need to round up as many warm bodies as we can in the next few days. This is coming whether we're ready or not."

Noah spat on the ground. "How many we think Kelly's crew has? Can't be that many if he's living way out in the sticks."

Victor shook his head again. "Your guess is as good as mine. Chuck seems to think we can handle them, but I ain't so sure."

Noah sighed, scratching his head. "When's Chuck want us to hit em?"

"One week, no more. He was damn clear about that."

"One week, one week," Noah muttered. "Not a lot of time to get prepared."

"I know, but Chuck's calling the shots," Victor said. "He wants blood and he wants it ASAP. Our asses are on the line here, so let's make it happen."

Noah pushed off the wall. "I hear you. I'll start rounding up every piece of trigger trash I can find. We'll be ready in time."

"Appreciate it," Victor said, clapping him on the shoulder. "Let's end this Kelly problem once and for all."

CHAPTER THIRTY
ABBY'S REDEMPTION

After the group's planning meeting broke up, Abby approached Claire, who was looking stern. Claire asked bluntly, "What do you want now?"

Abby said, "I heard Joe tell you and Miguel to head up the decoy team back at the cabin. You get to pick one more person and I'd like to volunteer for that spot."

Claire chuckled wryly. "Are you out of your mind?"

Abby responded, "Maybe, but I would like to prove myself a changed woman."

Claire shook her head firmly. "No way, get out of here. Go work on the garden committee or something else."

Abby looked at Claire, her eyes beginning to glisten with tears. "Claire, please, I want to prove to you and everyone that I can change. I can pull my weight. Please, I'm begging you."

Claire looked at her for a long moment, considering. Finally she said, "Grab your gear. We leave in fifteen minutes."

Abby thanked Claire profusely. "You won't regret this, Claire. I swear."

Claire's expression was doubtful. "We'll see."

The mid-morning Florida sun beat down on them mercilessly as Abby, Claire and Miguel hiked through the dense forest towards the cabin. Claire led the way, machete in hand, effortlessly slicing through the underbrush. Miguel brought up the rear, ever alert, his keen eyes continuously scanning their surroundings.

Abby struggled to keep up, sweat dripping down her face. The backpack full of supplies felt like it weighed a ton on her slender shoulders. Every muscle in her body screamed in protest but she gritted her teeth and pushed on, determined to prove herself.

After two grueling hours they reached the secluded cabin, nestled picturesquely alongside a flowing creek. Claire turned to Abby, eyebrow raised in grudging respect.

"Well, you made it. Let's get set up."

They entered the cabin and got to work fortifying it. Miguel set about boarding up windows and reinforcing weak spots while Claire took inventory of their supplies. Abby hovered nearby, eager to help.

Claire glanced at her. "Go collect some firewood. We'll need a fire going to make this look convincing."

Abby nodded and headed outside, gathering fallen branches and logs from the surrounding woods. The physical exertion felt good, cleansing. For the first time in a long while, she felt useful.

As the day progressed, the three fell into an easy rhythm. Miguel and Claire's skepticism seemed to fade as Abby competently followed their directions. By nightfall, the cabin was well-camouflaged and stocked. A cozy fire crackled in the hearth.

They ate a humble meal of canned beans and jerky as the sun dipped below the horizon. Miguel kept watch while Claire cleaned her rifle. Abby stared into the dancing flames, reflecting on the day's events.

She had endured the arduous hike, performed her tasks without complaint, and earned a modicum of trust. There was still a long way to go, but it was progress. For the first time since society collapsed, she felt a sense of purpose.

The next morning the sun filtered through the leafy canopy as Claire and Abby hiked deeper into the woods surrounding the cabin. Armed with wire, twine, and other trapping supplies, their mission was to set snares that would hopefully yield small game to supplement their provisions.

Claire led the way, machete swinging with practiced ease to clear a path through the dense underbrush. Abby followed close behind, trying her best to mimic Claire's surefooted grace but failing to mask the occasional stumble over protruding roots or stones.

After about fifteen minutes of walking, Claire stopped abruptly and crouched down next to a game trail, examining it closely. "This looks promising," she said. "You can tell it's frequently used by the tracks."

Claire began explaining how to construct a simple snare trap, demonstrating the process step-by-step. Abby watched intently, nodding along and asking the occasional question to clarify Claire's instructions.

"Now you give it a try," said Claire, handing Abby the materials. "Set one up over there along that trail."

Abby got to work, her brow furrowed in

concentration as she tried to replicate what Claire had just showed her. It took her a few attempts, but she eventually constructed a passable snare trap and secured it carefully across the narrow game trail.

"Not bad for your first time," Claire said appraisingly.

They continued through the woods, stopping periodically to place more snares. With each one, Abby grew a little more confident in her new skill. By the time they turned back towards the cabin, she had set several on her own under Claire's watchful eye.

"I think you've got the hang of this," said Claire. "We'll check them tomorrow and see if any of those snares were lucky."

Abby beamed at the hard-won praise. As they emerged from the tree line, she felt a swelling sense of accomplishment. For the first time in ages, she had proven useful, and earned a sliver of respect from someone she admired. There was still a long way to go to be fully accepted, but this small victory felt sweeter than any she had known in her previous life.

As Abby and Claire emerged from the tree line, the steady thwack of splitting wood rang out. Miguel was behind the cabin, his axe rising and falling in a steady rhythm as he worked to stockpile firewood. His sleeves were rolled up, revealing his muscular, sweat-sheened arms.

Seeing him hard at work, Abby immediately sprang into action. She rushed over to the freshly split logs, grabbing an armful and hoisting them up. Miguel paused mid-swing, eyebrow raised as Abby hustled past him towards the cabin, focused on her self-appointed task.

Claire walked up beside Miguel, amusement flickering across her face as she watched Abby disappear into the cabin with her load. Miguel turned to Claire, wiping his brow with the back of one calloused hand.

"So, she's really pulling her weight out there?" Miguel asked, a note of surprise in his gruff voice.

Claire nodded. "She is. I showed her how to set snares this morning. She picked it up quickly and set several on her own."

Miguel's eyes widened slightly at this revelation. He leaned on the axe handle and looked thoughtful for a moment.

"Huh," he grunted. "Maybe she is serious about making herself useful this time."

"Seems that way," Claire replied. "She kept up with me on the hike out there without a single complaint. And she's been working hard around here too."

Miguel glanced back toward the cabin just as Abby emerged again, her steps quick and purposeful.

"I'll be damned," he muttered under his breath. "Never thought I'd see the day."

Claire gave a small smile. "People can surprise you. Come on, let's give her a hand so we can all take a break."

Miguel nodded and set the axe aside. Together, they followed Abby's path back toward the wood pile, the steady trill of birdsong underscoring their footsteps.

That night Claire stared pensively into the crackling fire, watching the flames dance and twist. Abby sat across from her on the other side of the hearth, hands folded in her lap. The only sounds were the sporadic pops of burning wood and the muted chorus of crickets outside.

After several long moments, Miguel emerged from the back room, scratching his stubbled cheek and suppressing a wide yawn.

"Sorry ladies, but I'm bushed," he said gruffly. "I'm off to bed."

"Goodnight," Claire and Abby echoed in near unison. Miguel gave a tired wave and shuffled off down the hall.

An awkward silence descended on the two women left sitting by the firelight. Abby fidgeted slightly, smoothing her pants though there were no wrinkles.

Finally, Claire spoke up. "You know Abby, you did very well today. You picked up setting those snares pretty quickly. I guess it just goes to show, if you apply yourself you can accomplish anything."

Abby looked up, seeming genuinely surprised by the unprompted praise. "Well, thank you Claire," she said softly. "I guess that's always been the case, but maybe I was just applying myself to the wrong things. Things that I once thought were so important now seem very foolish when I look back on them." She paused, meeting Claire's gaze. "And I really want to thank you again for even giving me this chance."

Claire studied her for a moment before replying. "I'm gonna be honest with you, Abby, lay my cards on the table as it were. I see a change in you, but to be honest I'm still not sure if it's for real or if you're just playing another angle."

Abby nodded slowly. "I understand that, Claire, and I don't blame you. I know it will take time for me to regain trust, and I'm willing to wait. I know

I've been a bitch in the past, especially to you and Jojo. I'm sorry for that." She hesitated briefly before continuing. "I just hope I haven't done any permanent damage. Are you guys okay?"

"Yeah, I guess so," Claire said with a small shrug. "I mean, it's just so hard in this new world we're living in now. There's not a lot of alone time." She felt her cheeks flush slightly even as the words left her mouth.

Abby tilted her head, looking at Claire curiously. "I don't mean to pry, but..." Her voice trailed off.

"No, go ahead. What?" Claire prodded.

"Well, I was just curious...I mean, I was eavesdropping on you two when you were talking on the porch and told each other you had feelings for one another." Abby bit her lip. "And I will tell you now, I threw myself at Jojo after that and he totally turned me away. It really made me mad and, I dunno, I guess really jealous."

Claire raised her eyebrows in surprise. "Well, thank you for telling me that. Jojo did mention it, but refused to go into details. I appreciate you being honest." She took a slow breath before continuing. "But what is your question?"

"Wow, he's really grown a lot if he told you about that. He must really have strong feelings for you. I never thought he would be so open." Abby looked thoughtful. "I guess I'm just curious...how much has your relationship, uh..." She trailed off again.

"Uhm, what?" Claire pressed, though she had a good idea where this was headed.

"Uhm...how far has your relationship progressed?" Abby spoke the words in a rush, then looked sheepish. "You don't have to answer that. I'm not trying to sabotage anything, I'm just curious."

Claire couldn't help but chuckle. "Wow, right to the point, huh?" She shook her head, amused. "Well, to be honest, it hasn't progressed as far as we may like. I mean, given the circumstances we live in now, there's not a lot of alone time." She felt her face flush again. "Sure, we've stolen a few kisses, but that's really about it." She laughed lightly, surprised at herself for divulging even that much.

Abby looked thoughtful again. "Listen Claire, I'm saying this as your friend, and I truly am not trying to cause any trouble." She took a breath before continuing. "But trust me, it will be well worth the wait. Oh God, I can't believe I'm saying this to you, but Jojo is a very generous lover, if you know what I mean." She smiled sheepishly. "Trust me, it will all be worth it when it finally happens for you two.

And I truly hope that's soon."

Claire just stared wordlessly back at Abby for several long seconds, unsure how to respond. Finally she said slowly, "Wow...I don't really know what to make of that. I mean, I get what you're saying, but are we really becoming friends and confidants here? I'm still not totally sure I can trust you yet, Abby."

Abby met her gaze evenly. "I hope we're becoming friends, Claire. And I know you can't completely trust me yet - I get that. But I do want to be your friend and confidant, and I hope that happens in time. Please believe me that you can come to me if you need me."

Claire mulled over her words. "Thank you, Abby," she said finally. "I'll keep that in mind."

She stood, stretching her back. "I should get some rest too. See you in the morning Ab." Abby wished her a good night as Claire made her way down the hall, mind swirling with thoughts of trust, friendship, and the intriguing notion of intimacy with Jojo.

* * * * * * * * * * * * * * * * * * *

Dawn painted the horizon with strokes of fiery orange and blushing pink when Joe's sturdy boots crunched the gravel path leading to the cabin. His eyes, ever alert, scanned the surroundings, a mixture of concern and curiosity etched into the lines of his weathered face. The cabin stood solemnly, its wooden walls a silent testament to the chaos they'd all weathered.

Claire was outside, her blonde hair tied back in a no-nonsense ponytail, her movements graceful and purposeful as she checked their makeshift water filtration system. Joe approached, his footsteps announcing his presence before his voice did.

"Claire," he began, his tone carrying the weight of unspoken questions.

She straightened up and faced him, a hint of surprise flickering in her eyes before she nodded a greeting. "Joe. Up with the sun, I see."

He folded his arms across his chest. "I came by looking for Abby. Thought she'd skipped town again. But then someone mentioned you brought her here." His brows furrowed with concern. "Why?"

Claire exhaled softly, brushing a stray lock behind her ear. "I know it seems off-kilter. Abby... she pleaded with me. I was against it at first, but..." Her voice trailed off as she looked away momentarily.

Joe's gaze softened slightly. "Got to you, huh?"

"Yeah," Claire admitted with a reluctant nod. "I

actually started feeling sorry for her."

"Wow," Joe said, the word hanging between them like smoke from a snuffed-out flame. "I was certainly stunned when I found out."

Claire leaned against the wooden railing that bordered the cabin's porch. "She's been different so far — actually great," she confessed with cautious optimism. "Can't say I fully trust her yet, but Abby's been working hard to turn things around, change her image... and my mind."

Joe's eyes narrowed thoughtfully as he considered Claire's words.

"I just hope it continues," Claire finished with an earnest look in Joe's direction.

Joe gave a slow nod, taking in Claire's hopeful tone against his own reservations — a balancing act between skepticism and the possibility of genuine change.

"Yeah, let's hope so," Joe echoed, his voice a blend of skepticism and a reluctant hope. He shifted his weight from one foot to the other, casting a glance back toward the sun climbing its way up the sky. "Listen, the reason I came here is to go over the plans we've made with you guys, so you're totally prepared when — and if — this all goes down."

Claire straightened up, her attention sharpening

at the mention of preparations. Her gaze met his squarely, understanding the gravity of what they were about to discuss.

"I definitely want to go over this with you and Miguel," Joe continued, scratching at his beard—a habitual tell of his concern. "Should we include Abby in this conversation? I have to admit I'm still a bit skeptical of her loyalty; she really burned us last time." He paused, letting the weight of past betrayals hang in the air.

Claire pursed her lips, mulling over Joe's words. The quiet around them felt charged, every rustle in the underbrush louder in the silence.

"It's your call," Joe added after a moment. "I'll go with whatever you decide."

She exhaled slowly, knowing full well the risk of misplaced trust in times like these. Yet there was also the chance that Abby's intentions had indeed shifted.

Claire thought for a long moment, her gaze shifting between Joe and the ground as she weighed his words. Joe waited patiently, hands resting on his belt, his posture relaxed yet attentive.

Finally Claire spoke. "Yeah, what the hell. Let's give her a chance to prove her loyalty. It's probably the only way we're ever gonna know for sure."

Joe nodded, a flicker of cautious approval in his eyes. "Okay then, let's get everybody together and go over this."

Claire turned towards the cabin, hesitating before pulling open the weathered wooden door. "Abby," she called out. "Can you come out here for a minute? Joe wants to go over some plans with all of us."

There was a pause, then the sound of footsteps crossing the creaky floorboards inside. Abby emerged, her curvy figure on display in shorts and a midriff-baring top, her long blonde hair cascading over her shoulders. She offered Joe a tentative smile.

"Hey Joe. What's up?"

Joe's expression remained impassive. "Morning Abby. We've been working on a strategy for dealing with Chuck and his crew. Wanted to bring you in on it, get your thoughts."

Abby blinked, looking momentarily taken aback. "Oh. Wow, yeah, of course." She straightened up. "I really appreciate you including me. What can I do to help?"

Joe studied her for a long moment before giving a single nod. "Alright then. Let's grab Miguel and talk this through." He turned and started walking towards the edge of the property where Miguel could be seen splitting firewood, axe rising and falling in a steady rhythm.

Claire fell in step beside Joe while Abby trailed behind. As they approached Miguel, Joe called out, "Miguel, let's take a break on the wood for a bit. Got some plans to discuss that I want to go over with everyone."

Miguel embedded the axe in a tree stump and turned to face them, his expression impassive. "I'm listening," he said simply.

Joe glanced around at the group assembled before him, feeling the weight of leadership and a flicker of hope that maybe, just maybe, they could become a unified force strong enough to withstand whatever Chuck and his gang threw their way next.

Joe turned to face Abby, his expression stoic yet his eyes conveying a glimmer of compassion underneath his gruff exterior.

"Let me address the elephant in the room first, Abby," he began, his voice steady and solemn. "Are you truly with us now or are you still just looking out for yourself and staying loyal to Chuck?"

Abby blinked, looking startled by Joe's directness. She hesitated, glancing down as she nervously tucked her hair behind her ears. When she finally spoke, her voice was quiet but firm.

"Joe, I made a huge mistake. I thought I could manipulate Chuck and get my way, to be happy. I thought I could use my charms to have a great life filled with everything I ever wanted or needed." She shook her head ruefully. "I was a fool. I found out Chuck is pure evil."

Her voice caught and she looked away briefly before continuing. "I didn't want to get into this, but I think I need to tell you...after telling Chuck about you and Maria and Jojo and everything else, I thought he would reward me and make me his queen." She gave a hollow, mirthless laugh. "Stupid, right? But instead, he beat and raped me."

Claire's hand flew to her mouth in shock while Miguel's jaw tightened, his eyes flashing dangerously. Joe remained still, his gaze intent on Abby.

"It opened my eyes, Joe," Abby went on, her voice gaining strength. "As he was defiling me, I realized how stupid and selfish I had been. I'm so sorry for what I've done, but I promise you this - it will never happen again." Her expression grew fierce, her fists clenching at her sides. "And if I can help in bringing that monster down, I'm all in."

She fell silent, her chest rising and falling rapidly, raw emotion etched across her face. The others exchanged solemn glances, each processing Abby's revelation in their own way.

Finally Joe stepped forward, placing a gentle hand on Abby's shoulder. "I'm sorry that happened to you," he said gruffly. "And I appreciate you being honest with us." He gave her shoulder a light squeeze. "We'll make sure Chuck pays for what he's done. But right now, let's focus on keeping each other safe."

Abby nodded, hastily wiping away a tear. "Thank you," she whispered.

Joe gave a brisk nod then turned to address the whole group. "Now, about this plan..."

* * * * * * * * * * * * * * * * * * *

Joe proceeded to tell the three the plan they had come up with, which included allowing Chucks troops to get close to the cabin at which point they will detonate explosives at the rear line of Chuck's troops and simultaneously at the front line of his troops, basically trapping them in place and creating a kill zone. They will also detonate explosives in between the front and rear of their line as well and everyone will begin picking off his remaining men from treeline positions. They are currently in the process of burying claymores and other traps in place along the road that leads to the cabin. Claire, Miguel and Abby are impressed with the plan and ask what is their role? Joe says when it starts to hit the fan, they will need to hit the trees and start picking off as many of Chuck's men as they can. he also says, take no prisoners, eliminate them. Everyone agrees and Joe says he's heading back to the warehouse and tells them to be ready Chuck could come at any time.

Joe's boots crunched on the gravel driveway as he headed back to the path back to the warehouse , his mind racing with the preparations still needed before Chuck's forces arrived. Miguel followed him out, his brow furrowed with thought.

"Hey Joe, hold up a second," Miguel called out gruffly. Joe turned, regarding the other man with a questioning look.

"I know we gotta do what we gotta do to protect our own," Miguel said. "But this feels bigger than just you and Chuck settlin' a score. We take out his men, we're talkin' about a lot of lives ended."

Joe crossed his arms, his jaw tightening. "You got another option? Chuck's not gonna stop till he gets what he wants. We let him roll on in here, we're as good as dead."

Miguel nodded slowly, glancing back at the cabin where Claire and Abby were gathering supplies. "Yeah, I know. Ain't no good choices here. I just want to be sure we're doin' this for the right reasons, not just revenge."

"It ain't about revenge," Joe said firmly. "It's about survival. Protecting our family, our home. Sometimes you gotta fight to defend what's yours."

He put a hand on Miguel's shoulder. "I don't aim to kill anymore than I have to. But when Chuck gets here, it'll be a fight to the end. That's just how it's gotta be."

Miguel held his gaze for a moment before giving a grim nod. "Alright, I hear you. We'll do what we gotta do when the time comes."

They clasped hands briefly, a mutual understanding passing between them. Then Joe turned and headed off to continue preparations, hoping they'd be ready when Chuck's forces came marching in.

Joe's boots crunched rhythmically on the forest floor as he made his way back to the warehouse, lost in thought. Miguel's words weighed heavy, stirring an internal debate. Was he going too far, becoming the kind of ruthless man he once despised? But every time he pictured Abby, haunted and abused, or imagined Chuck's smug face, his resolve hardened.

This was about more than revenge. Chuck represented the kind of men who would take and take, who saw this lawless world as a chance to indulge their worst impulses without consequence. Joe had seen it before the EMP, the way men like Chuck exploited and destroyed without a second thought. Taking him down would tell others like him that there were still lines, still those willing to stand up no matter the cost.

Maybe Miguel was right, and there would always be someone eager to seize power, to rule through fear and violence. But stopping Chuck now would show that good people were willing to fight back. That they would defend their homes and families to the very end. Joe knew that decisive action now could save countless lives down the road.

As the warehouse came into view, Joe steeled himself, pushing aside any doubts. This was the only way, he was sure of it. They would be ready when Chuck came with his armies and weapons. And by ending this threat once and for all, they could start to build something better from the ashes. They could find hope again. Gripping his rifle tighter, Joe stepped inside, focused on the fight ahead.

CHAPTER THIRTY ONE
PAST AND PRESENT UNITE

The early morning sun cast a soft glow over the warehouse as Joe, surrounded by his trusted group, finalized their preparations for the inevitable confrontation with Chuck Warner's forces. Maria, her once smooth hands now callused and toughened by the recent days of hard labor, stepped up beside Joe. Her eyes, still gentle but with a new depth borne of resilience and pain, scanned the layout of their makeshift stronghold.

"Joe, if we're going to stand a chance against Chuck, we can't just think defensively," she said, her voice carrying the authority of someone who had seen the horrors of war both before and after the world as they knew it fell apart. "We need a medical station. Somewhere to triage and treat the injured when the time comes, because it will come."

Joe nodded gravely, looking to Paulette. Over

the last few days, she'd shown an uncanny knack for organizing and getting things done. "Paulette, do you think you can handle setting up a medical tent with Maria?"

Paulette's face grew determined. "You've got it, Joe. Maria's got experience in the field, and I know enough first aid to get by. We'll get it up and running."

So, amidst the sound of others loading ammo and laying traps, Maria and Paulette set to work. They chose a corner of the warehouse, with good light and close enough to spring into action but tucked away, to avoid being an easy target.

Maria, drawing upon her past as an army medic, began designating areas for various levels of care: one section for the critically wounded, another for those with less life-threatening injuries - all the way to a spot where those who merely needed rest could recover. She listed the supplies they'd need - bandages, disinfectant, painkillers, - most of which they scrounged up from the remnants of a ransacked pharmacy and from their own dwindling supplies.

With the help of some of the other women from the group, including a fierce young mother who'd lost too much to Chuck's greed, they set about sterilizing equipment and organizing medical tools with an efficiency that spoke of desperation and the need to feel useful in the face of oncoming violence.

Once the area was functional, Paulette stood at the entrance, arms crossed, reviewing their work. It wasn't a hospital, but it was something. Maria joined her, giving her a nod of satisfaction.

"We should run some basic first aid drills," Maria suggested. "Anyone who can stand should know how to apply a tourniquet or stitch a wound."

Paulette, who had proved an excellent teacher since the chaos began, agreed. "We start first thing tomorrow. Everyone needs to be ready for their role when Chuck comes. We won't let him think we're just waiting here defenseless."

Under Paulette's direction, they gathered the group and began training. Everyone took turns applying pressure dressings, splinting broken limbs with scraps of wood and duct tape, and even learning CPR. Given her past, Maria led some of the sessions, her face set in a mask of concentration as she corrected holds and wrapped bandages with experienced hands.

As dusk turned to night and the drills came to an end, a sense of shared purpose settled over the group. They had come from all walks of life but now found unity in their stand against a common enemy. Building their new life had not been without hardship, and they knew there was more to come. But as they looked around their temporary sanctuary, they knew they had built something together: not just a medical unit, but a community. And for Maria and Paulette, who had laid their doubts and past mistakes at the door of this fledgling medical facility, it was a testament to their unyielding spirit and the roles they had come to fill - as healers in the midst of chaos.

Paulette wiped the sweat from her brow as she surveyed the makeshift medical area one last time. Despite the looming threat of Chuck's forces, a swell of satisfaction rose in her chest. They had built something good here, something that would save lives when the battle came.

Maria stepped up beside her, hands calloused but steady. "We've come a long way," Paulette said, meeting her gaze. On an impulse, she added, "Wanna grab a drink? I think we've earned it after today."

Maria considered for a moment before a hint of a smile tugged at her lips. "Sure, I guess so. We certainly deserve it after all this."

They made their way to the quiet corner of the warehouse where Paulette kept her sparse belongings. From her pack she retrieved an unopened bottle of Vodka along with two shot glasses that caught the dim light.

Maria's eyebrows rose. "Wow, you really came prepared."

Paulette gave a wry chuckle as she poured them both a shot. "Comes from my Russian blood, I guess." She held up her glass in a toast. "To victory and freedom from Chuck and Za nashu druzhby."

Maria looking confused, "What does that last bit mean?"

Paulette smiles, "To our friendship."

"I'll certainly drink to all of that," Maria said, clinking their glasses before tipping back the Vodka. They both winced at the burn.

Paulette hesitated, then decided to be direct. "I hope you don't feel uncomfortable with me, Maria. I know I'm Joe's ex and you're his present. But I want us to be friends, and I hope we can be just that."

Maria considered her words. "I don't see why we can't be. I mean, I think you're over Joe, aren't you?"

"Absolutely," Paulette said fervently. "I've made a lot of mistakes in my life, and leaving Joe was one of the biggest. But I have moved on, please believe me. I'm not looking to get him back."

Maria nodded slowly. "I do believe you. And I have my own past I want to forget, as you've probably heard about. Mine may be more...severe. But I understand what you're saying." She gestured at the bottle. "How about another shot?"

Paulette smiled and refilled their glasses. "To new friends," she said, holding it up.

Their glasses clinked again. The liquid seared down their throats, sealing their newfound bond. Tomorrow they would face the battle together, side by side. But tonight, they took solace in forging an unexpected connection amidst the chaos.

CHAPTER THIRTY TWO
FORBIDDEN FEELINGS

With the amber hues of dusk painting the walls of the warehouse, Taylor found herself seeking solace in the quiet company of Jake as they sat atop a makeshift lookout at the far corner of the building. Below them, like busy ants, the rest of the group flitted about, each contributing to the stronghold's fortifications against the coming siege.

Jake adjusted the scope of his rifle, his eyes never straying far from the horizon. Taylor watched him, admiring the controlled calm he exuded despite the tension that wound tight in the air. Here was a man who spoke little, but whose actions reverberated with purpose and intent.

Taylor broke the silence, her voice a soft intrusion. "How are you holding up?"

Jake's gaze flicked towards her briefly before

returning to the scope. "As well as can be expected," he replied. "We've got a job to do, and I plan to do it."

Taylor nodded, wrapping her arms around her knees. "It's going to get dangerous, isn't it?"

Jake lowered his rifle, finally turning to lock eyes with her. "It is. But Chuck isn't going to walk away from this, not if I have anything to say about it."

Taylor couldn't help the shiver that ran through her at his words, the finality in his tone a stark reminder of the path laid out before them. "I trust you," she said earnestly, "I trust all of you to keep us safe."

Jake reached out, his hand resting over hers — a testament to the silent bond of trust they'd built. "We're gonna make it through this," he stated firmly.

The fading sun slipped beneath the edge of the earth, bathing the landscape in twilight's cool embrace. In that serene moment, Taylor let herself lean a little closer to Jake, drawing warmth from his solid presence.

Jake cleared his throat, a slight flush creeping up his neck. "We should check on the rest of the supplies before it gets too dark." His voice was steady but held a note of reluctance to leave the haven of their little perch.

Taylor nodded, standing and brushing off her pants. "Let's do it then. The sooner we're ready, the better."

Together, they descended the ladder, their steps in sync as they joined the chorus of activity below. The reality of their situation was a shadow on the horizon, dark and foreboding. But for Taylor and Jake, the fleeting comfort found in shared silence, the brush of hands and the harmonious step, served as an unspoken promise to stand guard over one another when darkness finally descended.

As they crossed the threshold into the warehouse, Taylor glanced over her shoulder at the rapidly darkening sky. The twilight was slipping away, and with it, the illusion of peace. She felt Jake's hand brush against hers once more, a quiet reassurance. They would face the night together, and when the dawn came, they would welcome it side by side.

The warehouse buzzed with the energy of their newfound community. People bustled about, focused on their tasks — a symphony of preparation and purpose. Within this web of activity, Alicia stood slightly apart, her eyes tracking the movements of Sam as he coordinated the loading of supplies into the back of a sturdy truck.

Sam's focused demeanor and sharp commands made her heart skip, admiration welling within her each time he effortlessly lifted a heavy crate or took a moment to explain something to one of the younger members. In Alicia's eyes, he was more than just a vital part of their defense committee — he was a man of action and strength, and she found herself drawn to him despite the chaos that brewed around them.

She observed, almost entranced, when one of the men approached Sam with a clipboard in hand, discussing the inventory with efficient clarity. Sam nodded, his hair catching the fading light as he turned to respond, his profile igniting something deep within Alicia that she'd never felt in the stark world before.

Stepping closer, desiring to be part of that world, Alicia found a reason to engage.

"Sam, do you need help with... anything?" Her voice was almost lost amidst the noises of logistics and survival.

Sam, turning to see who addressed him, gave her a friendly smile — a rarity amid the severity of recent days. "Ah, Alicia. You could actually help me go over the inventory list I have here. We can't afford mistakes."

Taking the list, Alicia worked through it with

Sam, close enough to catch the scent of woodsmoke and sweat that clung to him—a smell of work and dedication. As they confirmed numbers and checked boxes, she fought the urge to brush against his arm, to feel the solid reality of him.

Later, as dusk settled and the last light hovered like a delicate veil over the horizon, Alicia returned to the private quarters set up in the warehouse. Her mind buzzed with Sam's nearness, her cheeks flushed with her thoughts, and a timid hope that maybe—just maybe—he could feel something for her too.

It was a foolish notion, born of the adrenalin of survival and the closeness of shared danger, but it was a light in the dimness—a wondering, a whisper, that she cherished in the quiet of her own heart as she lay down to rest.

Unbeknownst to her, Sam also found himself thinking of Alicia that night. Her bravery in joining them, the quiet strength she'd shown, and the fleeting, tender moments they had shared checking off supplies. Could there be room for something more amidst the threat that loomed over them, not to mention she was only sixteen years old, in the old world that was a crime, but he was attracted to Alicia, could it really be wrong? This was a new world after all, so many questions to mull over.

But before that thought could take hold, the reality of their situation settled like a cold blanket over him, reminding him that the forthcoming confrontation with Chuck would not leave much space for tender affections. Right now, their survival was the only thing that mattered.

Sam sighed as he settled down for the few hours of sleep he could afford. There were those depending on him, counting on him to get them through the impending battle. Personal feelings had to wait. They had to.

CHAPTER THIRTY THREE
TEARS OF TRIUMPH

C laire and Abby trekked through the dense forest, eyes scanning the ground for signs of movement. The morning air was crisp, with faint wisps of mist swirling amongst the trees. Their boots crunched over fallen leaves and twigs as they made their way to the first snare. Claire crouched down, her athletic frame moving with practiced grace. Nothing. Just an empty wire loop.

They continued on, disappointment growing with each empty snare they encountered. By the third, Abby was ready to give up hope. Then she saw it - the unmistakable furry form of a squirrel dangling from a tree branch.

"Claire, come quick! We've got something!" Abby shouted.

Claire raced over, blonde ponytail swishing behind her. A wide grin spread across her face when she saw the squirrel caught in the cleverly fashioned snare.

"Nice job, Abby! This was one of yours, wasn't it?"

Abby nodded, beaming with pride. As Claire carefully removed the squirrel from the wire noose, Abby suddenly burst into tears.

Claire turned to her, confused. "It's okay, Abby. I know it's hard taking a life, but we need this to survive."

Between sobs, Abby choked out, "It's not that. I just can't believe I actually accomplished something real. For the first time in my life, I contributed without using my body or manipulating someone."

Understanding washed over Claire. She wrapped her arms around Abby, holding her shaking frame close.

"You did good, Abby. There's so much more you're capable of."

Abby clung to Claire, tears dampening her shirt. "Thank you for believing in me when I didn't even believe in myself."

After a moment, Claire pulled back, hands still grasping Abby's shoulders. "Come on, let's check the other snares. One squirrel won't go far, especially with Miguel's appetite."

Abby laughed through her tears. They set off again with renewed vigor. Luck was on their side - two more squirrels and a plump rabbit.

Claire holding up their catch "Hey let's get back to the cabin, we caught em', we'll let Miguel clean em' and we'll cook em.

As they trekked back, Abby halted, face suddenly serious. "Claire, I have a confession."

Claire stopped, concern creasing her brow. "What is it?"

"I don't have any recipes for cooking rabbit or squirrel," Abby deadpanned.

Claire rolled her eyes and chuckled. "You're something else, Ab, You are something else."

Claire and Abby returned to the cabin, fresh game in hand. Miguel looked up from the fire pit and smiled when he saw their catch.

"Well, looks like we're eating good tonight," he said.

The girls walked up and held out the squirrels and rabbit. "Yes, we'll eat very well tonight as soon as you clean these bad boys, big bro," Claire said with a grin.

Miguel nodded. "You bet, lil' sis. I'll get right on it. How do you wanna cook 'em - chop the meat for a stew or roast 'em whole over the fire?"

Claire pondered for a moment before responding. "How about you chop up the squirrel meat into chunks and we'll make a stew. We can stretch it into a meal for tomorrow too. Let's roast the rabbit over the open flame."

"I like that idea. Consider it done," Miguel said as he took the animals and prepped his cleaning area.

Claire nodded in satisfaction then turned to Abby. "I'm gonna head down to the stream and get cleaned up. I feel filthy after tromping around the woods all morning. You wanna join me for a bath?"

Abby eagerly agreed. "Absolutely, I could definitely use a good scrub after today. Nothing better than a brisk dip to wash off the grime."

The two women grabbed spare clothes and towels. As they walked off, Miguel called out "Don't wander too far now. Holler if you need anything."

Claire waved in acknowledgement. The promise of a refreshing bath lifted their spirits as they bantered back and forth on the short hike to the stream.

As Claire and Abby made their way to the stream, the cool water seemed a blissful promise after the morning's exertions. They laid their spare clothes and towels on the rocks, stripping down to nothing with a modesty borne of companionship rather than embarrassment. Slipping into the stream, they submerged themselves with sighs of relief, the sun-warmed surface layer giving way to the invigorating chill beneath.

The stream was a balm to both body and spirit, as they lathered with bars of soap, washing away the sweat and grime. The open sky above them served as a canopy to their laughter as they splashed, momentarily freed from the weight of their plight.

It was Claire who first noticed the disturbance — a shift in the dense brush on the far bank of the stream, slight but out of place. She stilled, her hand stilling Abby's, and nodded silently towards the other side. Instinctively, they sank lower into the water, the current a cool kiss on their sun-kissed shoulders as they peered across the rippling surface.

Abby's heart rate quickened as her eyes scanned the far bank, her previous ease evaporating into the crisp air. "Do you think — could it be one of Chuck's scouts?" she whispered, her voice barely carrying above the gentle babble of the stream. The fear of being discovered, vulnerable and exposed, clenched in her gut.

Claire shook her head slightly, unsure. "Could be," she murmured back, "Or it could be a deer, or some small critter."

They waited, breaths held, as the foliage shivered once more. There was a tension in the air now, each rustle a potential threat. Then, without warning, a rabbit burst forth from the undergrowth, bounding with startled white-tailed haste across the clearing. Both women exhaled, their laughter mingling with relief's music.

"False alarm," Claire said, grinning at Abby, who rolled her eyes — embarrassed but glad for the error.

They finished their bathing swiftly after that, the moment of levity a bright flare against the backdrop of their grim situation. Dressing quickly, they made their way back to the cabin, a forged closeness between them like the unseen currents running beneath the stream's skin. Though it had been a false alarm this time, they were acutely aware that Chuck's forces were out there — somewhere — and the stakes were as high as ever.

CHAPTER THIRTY FOUR
SCOUTING REPORT

The trading post's door creaked open, cutting through the chatter and clinking of wares. Noah stepped inside, eyes sweeping the dimly lit interior, where merchants and travelers bartered over goods and gossip. He found Victor in the corner, leaning over a crate, his gaze locked on a rusted compass.

"Victor."

Victor looked up, a smile creasing his weathered face. "Noah, there you are. Let's step outside."

The pair emerged into the bright daylight, the clamor of the post fading behind them as the door swung shut.

"How did it go?" Victor asked, squinting against the sun.

"No sweat," Noah replied, dusting off his jacket. "I found the cabin right where the bimbo said it would be."

"Good," Victor nodded. "And how hard is this gonna be?"

"It should be like taking candy from a baby. There weren't many people there that I could tell. The place isn't big enough to house any huge number of people and there were no encampments around the place. We should be able to march right in and take over with ease."

Victor exhaled a long breath, relief washing over his features. "You have no idea how relieved I am to hear that. Chuck has been on my ass day and night; he wants these people dealt with. He's been fuming. Listen, when we make our move on this cabin, we cannot harm his wife. He wants her brought to him; I think he has some pretty unpleasant plans for her." He shuddered slightly. "He is one sick dude; he scares the crap out of me."

Noah's lips curled into a half-smile. "I know what you're saying boss." He paused for a moment before adding, "What about the blonde bimbo? I wouldn't mind having a go at that myself."

Victor shot him a sharp look. "No, you better bring her back untouched as well. As a matter of fact, we had better bring back any attractive women to the post; I think Chuck wants to get them all working for him if you know what I mean."

The two men shared a knowing glance before parting ways, each lost in their own thoughts about the impending raid and its vile intentions orchestrated by Chuck Warner—a man whose presence loomed even in his absence.

* * * * * * * * * * * * * * * * * * *

Victor found Chuck in his office, leaning back in a worn leather chair as he gazed out the dirty window. Chuck didn't turn as Victor entered, simply lifting a hand in lazy acknowledgement.

"It's all coming together," Victor said, coming to stand beside the desk. "The cabin is lightly defended just as we thought. Mostly women and children by the looks of it."

Chuck turned his cold eyes on Victor. "And Maria? She's there?" His voice was flat, devoid of emotion.

Victor nodded. "Oh yes. Right where our source said she'd be."

Chuck's mouth curled into a cruel smile. "Good, good. You're bringing her back alive now, yes? Unharmed?"

"Of course," Victor reassured him. "Strict orders

- the men know she's to be captured alive."

Chuck nodded approvingly. "And the other women?"

Victor smiled thinly. "Any that catch the men's eyes will be brought back too. I know how you like to...take advantage of such opportunities."

Chuck barked out a laugh. "Good man. Always thinking ahead in my best interests." His amusement faded. "So when does this all go down?"

"Day after tomorrow," Victor replied promptly. "The men are prepping gear today, and we'll finalize plans tonight. We've got over a hundred men now, so overpowering the place will be child's play."

Chuck grinned wolfishly. "Perfect. I want my wife back by nightfall." His eyes glinted with malicious excitement. "That bitch has much to atone for. I've waited a long time for this."

Victor nodded, a flicker of unease in his eyes. "Yes sir. We'll take care of it." He turned and left the office, a knot in his stomach at the thought of what awaited Maria and the other women when Chuck's cruel hands closed around them once more.

Chuck remained seated calmly in his worn leather chair, staring out the filthy window pane as his thoughts turned to Maria. A slow, cruel smile spread across his weathered face as he envisioned having her back under his control once more.

Oh, she would pay dearly for leaving him all those years ago. He would force her back into prostitution, peddling her body to every wretched lowlife in Center Hill. They would line up around the block for a turn with the infamous Maria Warner, wife of the notorious Chuck Warner. Her allure would be irresistible - the broken woman who once belonged to the most feared man in town.

Chuck's smile widened, his eyes glinting with malicious glee. Yes, he would take great pleasure in parading Maria around like a prize pony, whoring her out night after night. The money would flow endlessly into his coffers. And Maria - ha! She would be shattered, reduced to a whimpering, compliant plaything desperate to avoid his wrath. Chuck exhaled a satisfied sigh at the thought. This was going to be even sweeter than he imagined.

Soon Maria would be delivered back into his clutches, ready for him to torment and violate however he wished. Chuck could hardly wait to see the defiant light leave her eyes, to watch her spirit crumble once and for all. His heart raced with anticipation. She had escaped him once, but not this time. This time, she would never leave his side again.

CHAPTER THIRTY FIVE
THE CALM AND THE STORM

Dusk settled over the warehouse, its looming shadow stretching across the cracked pavement where Joe and Maria found respite on an old bench. The air was cool, carrying the scent of pine and the distant murmur of the wilderness that bordered their makeshift stronghold. Joe's hands were rough, calloused from days spent fortifying defenses and nights cleaning his guns. They fidgeted with a piece of wire he'd twisted into various shapes, a habit he'd developed when his mind raced.

He glanced at Maria, noting how the fading light played in her ponytail. "Maria," he started, his voice a low rumble against the encroaching silence of the night, "you think we've covered all our bases? We ready for what's coming?"

Maria met his gaze, her eyes reflecting the

steeliness of her resolve. "Joe, we've done more than most could with half the time. The road's mined. We've got our infirmary, supplies are piling up... Everyone's drilled into the plan. We're as set as we'll ever be."

Joe's eyes didn't waver, but his hands stilled. "Hope you're right. It's just... what if we missed something?"

"There will always be 'what ifs,'" Maria countered with a gentle firmness that belied her calm exterior. "At some point, you've got to trust your instincts to handle those moments."

He hesitated before voicing his deeper concern. "It's just... Look, I don't mean any disrespect, but aside from a couple of us guys here—"

Maria cut him off with a knowing look. "Because what?"

He exhaled heavily. "These women... they've been through hell already. Are they really up for a fight?"

Maria's expression softened yet carried an undeniable strength. "Joe, these women have stared down their own nightmares with Chuck Warner at the helm. Fear might grip some, but I've seen fire in their eyes too—fire for justice, for revenge. Trust them to fight for a life far removed from Warner's shadow."

His gaze locked onto hers, a mix of admiration and something deeper shimmering between them. "Maria... I love you more than I've ever known possible. You're my cornerstone." He leaned closer, voice dropping to a whisper charged with emotion. "When this is all over... just be ready."

Maria raised an eyebrow, a hint of amusement playing on her lips. "Ready for what, pray tell?"

Joe cleared his throat, suddenly feeling bashful. "You know..."

"No Joe, I have no idea," Maria said coyly. "Tell me."

Joe's face flushed. He stared at the ground, scuffing his boot against a crack in the pavement. "Be ready to...you know, be made love to. Like you've never been made love to before."

Maria tilted her head, regarding Joe with an expression he couldn't quite read. Then she reached out and lifted his chin so their eyes met. "Oh, I'm definitely ready for that," she said, her voice low and throaty.

Joe's breath caught in his chest. He'd never heard her speak like that before. His heart hammered as he noticed the way the fading light illuminated her lips. Unable to resist, he leaned in and kissed her deeply. Maria responded in kind, the world around them fading away.

When they finally broke apart, both were panting slightly. Joe brushed a strand of hair from Maria's face, his fingers lingering on her cheek. "I love you, Maria."

Maria covered his hand with her own. "I love you too, Joe. So much that it scares me sometimes." She nuzzled against his palm. "But it also gives me strength, knowing you'll be by my side, no matter what happens."

Joe pulled her close, holding her against his chest as the first stars began to peek out in the darkening sky. Neither spoke, content to let the moment stretch on, warmed by each other's presence as the night embraced them.

As night claimed its domain over the sky above them, Joe and Maria held onto each other—their embrace sealing their shared determination to see through the darkness ahead.

* * * * * * * * * * * * * * * * * * *

The horizon blazed with a fiery hue as dawn clawed its way above the dense line of pines surrounding the warehouse. Joe stood sentinel on the makeshift rampart, a steaming mug clasped in his hands, its warmth seeping into his calloused skin. He mulled over the plans etched in his mind's eye, tracing and retracing each step like a mantra.

A disturbance shattered the morning calm as Sam burst into view, sprinting with an urgency that sent a shiver down Joe's spine. Gasping for air, Sam delivered the news, "This is it, we've got incoming, looks like about a hundred men heading straight down the road towards the cabin."

Joe's eyes narrowed, a slow nod acknowledging the gravity of the moment. "This is it." He turned to find Maria, her presence grounding amidst the surge of adrenaline. "Tell Sarah to run to the cabin. Warn Claire, Miguel, and Abby—Chuck's men are incoming."

Without hesitation, Maria sprinted off to find Sarah while Joe's voice boomed across the compound. "Positions! Everyone to your stations!"

Jojo and Jake vanished into the forest's embrace, their silhouettes blending with the underbrush as they settled into their concealed nests. The air hummed with tension, a palpable electric charge that pulsed through the group.

Maria located Sarah with swift precision. "To the cabin—now! Warn them!"

Sarah nodded, determination etched on her features as she plunged into the woods' dappled shadows. The trees swallowed her whole as she became one with the natural labyrinth leading to safety.

Back at the warehouse, Joe's commands continued to fly as he marshaled his forces with practiced ease. "Eyes sharp! We hold our ground!"

Maria and Paulette transformed their quarters into a bastion of healing, bracing for what was to come. Their hands moved with purpose as they stocked supplies and fortified their sanctuary.

The women who had known suffering at Chuck's behest melted into the forest alongside Joe's seasoned warriors—a vengeful whisper among rustling leaves. They carried their scars as armor and their fury as weapons.

Joe turned to Sam once more, seeking any scrap of advantage they might glean from his scouting report. "How long was their column?"

"Not very long at all, Joe," Sam replied with a cautious optimism that did little to lighten Joe's stony visage. "They looked to be a very disorganized and undisciplined bunch."

A ghost of a smile touched Joe's lips before vanishing like smoke. "I like the sound of that," he conceded. "But let's not get too overconfident—anything can happen; anything can go wrong. If it does, we'll just have to adjust on the fly."

Sam gave a resolute nod before both men turned their gaze toward the road that would soon bring Chuck's army to their doorstep. They stepped in unison toward destiny's uncertain embrace—ready for whatever hellfire would rain upon them.

Dawn's gentle glow was deceptive, promising tranquility where none would be found. The Kelly family and their allies lay in wait, tension singing in their veins as they readied for the battle that would determine their fates. Joe's eyes flicked to the treeline, then to the road, and finally to the sky—each glance a silent prayer that their preparations would be enough.

In the quiet before the storm, Joe's voice cut through the silence. "Remember, let the blasts be our signal. When you hear it, unleash everything you've got. No mercy." His words were a steel cable binding them all to the task at hand.

Nestled in his perch, Jojo clutched his rifle, the weight familiar and oddly comforting. Jake mirrored his position on the opposite side of the road, each man an anchor point for the defense. Their eyes met across the expanse, a silent vow passing between them.

Miguel and Claire making their way from the cabin lay in wait closer to the road, their bond as siblings an unspoken advantage in this deadly dance. They exchanged a look—one of determination mixed with fear—before focusing on their designated sectors.

Abby lingered in her hiding spot, a smirk playing on her lips despite the danger. She had no love for Chuck or his men and relished any chance to show Jojo she could be more than just a pretty face.

Maria's fingers brushed over her weapon with a lover's touch. The cold metal was unforgiving but reliable—a stark contrast to her estranged husband whose men marched toward their demise.

A distant rumble signaled Chuck's army drawing near—a monstrous cacophony of shuffling feet and laughter that shattered any remaining illusion of peace. Sam was right, these guys were way too confident and completely unaware of what was about to be unleashed on them. Joe raised his hand, signaling his forces to steady themselves.

Joe waited as the group of men grew nearer, timing was everything. He wanted to take out as many as possible with the first blasts, hitting them at the front of the column as well as the rear at the same time. As he waited he scanned the men in search of their leader Chuck, but he was not to be found, it seemed another man at the front of the column was in charge, Chuck was a no-show.

Finally Joe was satisfied that the men were in the perfect position and the first explosion erupted at the front of the column, quickly followed by a second at the rear—a crescendo of fire and earth that tore through Chuck's front line with merciless efficiency. It was as if thunder had clapped its hands right there on the ground.

"Now!" Joe's command was lost in another explosion as he and Sam fired into the chaos. The air crackled with gunfire as Joe's forces executed their plan with ruthless precision.

Chuck's men scattered like ants from a disturbed hill—panic overtaking strategy as they sought escape from the unexpected onslaught. Some veered off-road only to be met by secondary explosions that rocked the woods, turning their refuge into another layer of hell.

Maria picked off stragglers with sharpshooter precision while Claire and Miguel provided more firepower, their movements synchronized by years of protecting one another.

Amidst gunfire and cries, Abby surprised

herself with her own calm amidst chaos—each shot she took steadier than she'd ever imagined herself capable of.

As Chuck's army buckled under Joe's well-orchestrated attack, it became clear that retreat was not an option for them. The woods offered no safety; only further disarray awaited those who fled from Joe's wrath.

Joe scanned the battlefield from his vantage point—a general overseeing his troops—with pride swelling in his chest at their unwavering courage. They had become more than family; they were warriors fighting for a future free from tyranny.

And as smoke billowed into the sky, mingling with the dissipating fog of dawn, Joe Kelly knew this was but one battle in a war they could not afford to lose.

* * * * * * * * * * * * * * * * * * *

A haze of gunpowder and dust lingered in the air, the stench of spent ammunition and sweat mingling in the aftermath. Joe stood, rifle still at the ready, scanning the tree line with a hawk's gaze. The last echoes of gunfire had died down, leaving an eerie silence in their wake.

"Is everyone alright? Anyone need medical attention?" His voice cut through the stillness, a beacon for his scattered family.

The practiced drill kicked in without hesitation. "Number one, okay!" Sam's voice came first, strong and unshaken.

"Number two, okay!" Jojo's response followed, his tone as steady as his aim had been moments before.

One by one, they called out their numbers. "Number three, okay!" Jake chimed in, relief coloring his voice.

"Number four, okay!" Claire's affirmation was crisp and confident.

Each call was a note in a symphony of survival, culminating in Miguel's gruff "Number five, okay!" which rolled over the terrain like distant thunder.

Joe exhaled a breath he didn't realize he'd been holding. His crew had weathered the storm intact. "Mop up and be careful," he commanded next.

The group descended upon the scene with grim determination etched into their features. Sam moved with a soldier's precision, checking pulses and ensuring threats were neutralized. Jojo mirrored his actions on the opposite side of the road, his expression stone-like as he carried out the necessary brutality.

Jake followed suit, each movement deliberate and necessary; his face was a mask of stoic resolve. Claire stepped lightly between bodies, her athletic form belying the gravity of her task as she made sure none of their assailants would rise again.

Miguel brought up the rear. His scar seemed to pull tight across his cheek as he performed his duty—each pull of the trigger a necessary evil to protect what was left of their humanity in this harsh new world.

Together they worked under Joe's watchful eye until each fallen enemy lay still in eternal silence. It was cruel work—necessary but soul-rending—and it bonded them further as family forged by fire and blood.

Maria edged closer to Joe, her eyes scanning the clearing, a mirror of his own vigilance. "Joe, he wasn't with them," she said, her voice low, "I never saw Chuck."

Joe nodded, the grip on his rifle never wavering as he kept watch. "Yeah, I took note of that as well. What a coward, sending these men out to do his dirty work and staying behind safe and sound."

Maria's brow furrowed with concern. "What are we gonna do? He's just going to keep coming with more men."

Joe turned to her, the resolve in his eyes as clear as the determination in his stance. "I agree we need to cut the head off this snake — and sooner rather than later. I have a feeling this was the bulk of his men. I think he's probably at his weakest point right now and the good news is, he doesn't even know it yet." Joe's gaze shifted back to the horizon. "I think we need to make some quick plans and go after that bastard before he can do more damage."

Maria nodded, her expression hardening with the prospect of what was to come. She knew Joe was right; they couldn't wait for Chuck to strike again. The time for action was now.

Joe called everyone together, his expression grim yet resolved. "It doesn't look like Chuck was among these men," he stated flatly. "We need to make plans to head back to Center Hill and deal with him for good. We have an advantage right now since Chuck's unaware his forces are dead. I believe this was the bulk of his men - he probably only has a small security force left protecting him."

He scanned the group, making sure all eyes were on him. "We need to move fast, before he realizes his men aren't coming back. I know it's going to take time to clean up this mess on the road," he said, glancing at Jojo who nodded in agreement. "But we'll have to deal with that when we get back. If we head out now, we can be there by nightfall and plan an attack for the morning."

Joe's eyes settled on Abby. "I hate to ask this, but Abby, do you think you could organize some of the women to start cleaning up this road? It's a damn dirty job, but it'll only get worse as the bodies start to decay."

Abby met his gaze unflinchingly. "Absolutely, Joe. We'll get it done."

"Make sure to take any weapons, ammo, or useful items you find on them," Joe reminded her.

"Yes sir," Abby replied, already turning to head back and gather help from the warehouse.

Joe's attention shifted back to the core group. "Okay, Jojo, Sam, Jake, Claire, Miguel - let's move out!"

Maria stepped forward, her brow furrowed. "What about me?"

Joe hesitated. "Maybe you could help Abby?"

"No way, Joe," Maria said firmly. "I want in on killing that bastard. There's no way I'm staying behind."

Joe looked defeated but nodded. "Okay, I get it. Let's all grab some gear and get moving on the road in ten minutes."

The group dispersed to gather supplies, determination etched on their faces. In minutes they had reconvened, armed and ready. Joe took one last look at the carnage behind them, then set his sights on the road ahead. It was time to end this, once and for all.

CHAPTER THIRTY SIX
A PLEASANT DIVERSION

Chuck Warner perched at the edge of his leather chair, the weight of his thoughts creasing the lines around his eyes. His office, a sanctum of polished wood and subdued light, hummed with the silence of anticipation. Shadows danced across his face as he peered out the window, eyes tracing an invisible path across the landscape.

Calculations ticked through his mind like a metronome, each beat a step closer to Maria. The invading force had marched at dawn; their boots would now be stirring dust on the horizon, drawing a noose around that secluded cabin.

His fingers drummed against the mahogany desk, each tap a tick of the clock, a moment closer to reunion and victory. "They should make camp by dusk," he murmured to himself, picturing them—a relentless tide of strategy and strength—poised for the morrow's assault.

Rest would be brief; they were men molded by his will, driven by his command. As morning light pierced through darkness, so would they pierce through any resistance that Joe and his pitiful band could muster.

He rose from his chair and walked to a decanter perched on a side table, poured amber liquid into a glass but didn't drink. His gaze wandered back outside, thinking on that distant cabin where Maria defied him with her presence.

"They'll have her back by tomorrow night," he whispered to himself, "or by midday the next day at the latest." A surge of control washed over him; patience was a game he played well. He set down the untouched glass and returned to his chair.

Chuck Warner could wait, but a little company while he waited would certainly help take the edge off.

Chuck flicked his wrist, a silent command. Moments later, the door creaked open and one of his four personal guards, a mountain of a man named Griffin, stepped inside. His presence filled the doorway, dark eyes trained on Chuck with unwavering attention.

"Yes sir?"

Chuck leaned back in his chair, a picture of casual authority. "We acquired that pretty young thing the other day," he started, steepling his fingers, "and I've been remiss in welcoming her to our little family." His lips curled into a smile that didn't quite reach his eyes. "Bring her to me. Make sure she's cleaned up first and smelling nice. I'm in the mood to celebrate tonight."

Griffin's expression remained stoic, betraying no thoughts on the command he'd been given. "Yes sir, right away."

As Griffin turned on his heel and exited the office, Chuck's smile broadened. He imagined the girl's face—freshened up and pretty—a welcome sight for sore eyes. The past few days had been a taut string of strategy and waiting, each hour stretching longer than the last.

He allowed himself a moment to relish in the anticipation of the evening's diversion. Chuck needed this—a gentle reminder of the power he wielded not just over armies and territories but over people too. It was a subtle form of celebration but an effective one; an assertion of control as much as it was an indulgence.

The thought warmed him like a sip of fine

whiskey, smoothing out the edges of his relentless drive with the promise of soft curves and compliant whispers. Chuck's gaze drifted back to the window, watching as dusk began to paint the sky with strokes of fiery orange and purple.

Tonight would be good—a respite woven into the fabric of conquest and ambition. Chuck Warner allowed himself that small concession to humanity amid the grand chess game he orchestrated from this room where futures were decided with the clink of glass and stroke of pen.

In less than an hour, Griffin's knuckles rapped against the mahogany door with military precision, a metronome's echo through the corridors of Chuck Warner's personal quarters. A single wave from Chuck summoned him inside. The room, steeped in shadow and anticipation, brightened as Griffin stepped aside, revealing the girl.

Robbin hesitated at the threshold, her wide eyes drinking in the opulence around her. The dim light in the room played across her features, revealing a natural beauty untouched by artifice.

Chuck appraised her with a gaze both approving and calculating. "Definitely worth the wait," he thought, a silent toast to his impeccable taste. With a gesture smooth as silk, he beckoned her forward and dismissed Griffin with an indifferent flick of his wrist.

"Welcome, my dear," Chuck's voice wrapped around Robbin like velvet. "Make yourself at home and feel comfortable." He gestured toward the plush seating area. "Do you like whiskey?"

"I've never had any," she replied, her voice a soft tremor in the grand room.

"Well then, you're in for a real treat." Chuck poured a golden stream into a glass, his movements deliberate. "This is some damn fine whiskey." He handed her the glass with a charismatic smile. "Drink up, but slowly, my dear. Just sip it at first."

She followed his instruction, tentative lips brushing against the rim of the glass.

"What's your name, sweetie?" Chuck eased into his role as gracious host.

"My name is Robbin."

"Robbin," he savored her name as if it were another fine spirit. "I wanted to take this opportunity to formally welcome you to our little family here." His eyes remained fixed on her as he spoke. "Have you enjoyed yourself so far?"

She shifted uncomfortably under his scrutiny. "Well... I've enjoyed having food to eat and safety — not having to be out on the streets. It's very scary out there."

"Ahhh yes," Chuck nodded, feigning empathy while his mind worked like clockwork. "I'm glad we could provide that for you. But you know nothing comes for free."

"I understand that." Robbin clasped her hands together in front of her as if seeking warmth from their touch. "I need to contribute for my keep. I can cook and clean; I'm a pretty good cook."

"Yes, we may need you to help out with those tasks for sure." Chuck rose from his seat and began to close the distance between them. "But Robbin, I think you can contribute in an even more valuable way as well."

Her eyes widened with dawning realization as she took an involuntary step back. "How is that?"

"Well, Robbin my sweet," Chuck circled behind her like a predator eyeing its prey, "you have certain assets that I think people would pay a great deal to enjoy."

"I don't know what you mean." Her voice wavered; uncertainty laced each word.

Chuck's shadow fell over her as he leaned in close enough for his breath to feather across her skin. "Before we use those assets, Robbin," he said, voice dropping an octave, "I'll need to look them over for myself and make sure you know what you're doing." His fingers traced the neckline of her dress with feigned tenderness that belied his true intent. "We certainly wouldn't want any unhappy clients now would we?"

"I think I'd prefer to stick to cooking and cleaning," she stammered.

"But my dear," Chuck's words were honeyed steel as he drew closer still, "you have so much more to give."

Robbin's dress fell away in slow motion—a cascading fabric waterfall—revealing trembling shoulders bathed in soft light.

"Now let's just make sure what we're working with here." His voice was rough-hewn granite now; command etched into every syllable.

Robbin began to sob softly, shoulders shaking like leaves in an unforgiving wind.

"Take the rest off my dear." Robbin hesitated and pleaded, "Do it," he urged with growing impatience. "Now."

Her compliance came through tears and tremors as she shed the last vestiges of cloth between them.

Chuck's grin was all sharp edges—a predator baring teeth—as he appraised her fully now laid bare before him.

"Yes... I think you will do just fine." His eyes gleamed with dark promise. "But of course, I will need to make sure you're up to the job—with a little test run."

CHAPTER THIRTY SEVEN
SHOWDOWN AT LAST

Amber hues bled from the sky, surrendering to the inky embrace of twilight as Joe's group nestled into the wooded fringe of Center Hill. They had reached their destination with the stealth of shadows, the looming trading post just a whisper away.

Sam's silhouette melted into the underbrush, his departure barely a rustle against the evening's breath. The rest of the group, worn from the day's trek, took Joe's advice to heart, finding solace in sleep's ephemeral escape. But for Joe and Maria, rest was a stranger in these hours.

They lay side by side on a bed of earth and fallen leaves, their proximity a silent conversation in itself. Joe turned his head slightly toward Maria, his voice low but firm. "After Chuck's gone, we gotta think about what comes next. Can't leave a hole someone else will fill."

Maria nodded, her ponytail brushing against her back as she propped herself on an elbow. "The town needs someone with integrity... Someone to keep the peace."

"We can help set that up," Joe suggested, "Train some folks. They gotta learn to stand on their own."

Their whispers wove through the night until sleep claimed them too, granting a temporary reprieve from the weight of their mission.

In those small hours when night hesitates before yielding to dawn, Sam returned like a ghost from his reconnaissance. The others stirred as he recounted his findings.

"Four guards," Sam said with quiet confidence. "We can take 'em out without a sound if we're smart about it."

Joe rose, muscles protesting mildly as he processed Sam's intel. "Let's figure out how to quietly handle those guards."

Sam sketched out the scene with his hands as if painting an invisible canvas. "One guard each side. Use cover and stay low. Knives only."

Joe nodded in agreement. "Perfect. We move now while darkness is our ally."

With their plan set and resolve hardened like steel

in fire, they readied themselves to reclaim Center Hill from its would-be kingpin. The quiet before action thickened around them as they stepped into the shadows, guardians of a dawn yet unseen.

Leaves crunched softly underfoot as the group fanned out, spectral figures gliding through the night's embrace. Joe and Maria slipped toward the north side of the trading post, their movements deliberate, a choreography refined by necessity. The north guard stood with his back to them, unaware of the impending storm.

On the south side, Claire and Miguel melded with the darkness. Their bond as siblings lent them a silent language of nods and gestures. Miguel's hand signaled 'wait,' his eyes locked on the oblivious guard's routine patrol.

Jojo and Jake huddled against the west wall. Jojo's beret was a shadow atop his head, his gaze unwavering as he counted down with his fingers— three... two... one.

Eastward, Sam was a solitary wraith, his presence unknown to Griffin, who took lazy puffs of a cigarette. The orange glow briefly illuminated Griffin's face before Sam struck, a silent predator. The blade flashed in a swift arc, and Griffin crumpled without fanfare.

Simultaneously, Joe and Maria closed in on their target. Joe's hand clasped over the guard's mouth as Maria's blade found its mark beneath the jawline. The guard slumped against Joe, who eased him to the ground with care to avoid any sound.

Claire watched Miguel's back tense before he darted forward, a panther pouncing on its prey. His arm snaked around the southern guard's neck; there was a brief struggle before silence reigned once more.

On the west side, Jojo made his move, his approach a whisper against the night. Jake stood sentry as Jojo disabled their guard with swift efficiency—a testament to training that never dulled.

With each fallen adversary, the group's path cleared like mist at sunrise. They converged silently at their designated meeting point near the entrance of the trading post—their unity a quiet triumph in the shroud of night.

Dawn flirted with the horizon, casting tentative light over the scene as Joe's commands issued in hushed tones. "Sam, take the back. Claire, you and Mig watch those windows. Jojo, Jake—side exits. Nobody gets out but us." They nodded, each melting away to their posts, shadows within shadows.

Maria stood firm, her gaze unwavering. "I'm

going with you, Joe."

He studied her for a moment before nodding once. "Alright, but stay sharp."

Together they crossed the threshold of the trading post, the door's hinges obliging their silent entry. Room by room they swept through the space, Joe leading with Maria a vigilant echo at his side. The stillness of the building was a stark contrast to the adrenaline coursing through their veins.

Each empty room they left behind tightened the coil of tension between them. The last door loomed ahead, its unremarkable facade belying the potential encounter within.

Joe's hand paused on the knob before turning it with deliberate care. It gave way, it was unlocked. The door swung open to reveal the room's occupants in repose on an old mattress. Joe's eyes locked onto two nude figures, one a young woman and the other most definitely was that of Chuck Warner, his chest rising and falling in deep sleep next to the young woman whose identity was unknown to them.

Joe's stance became granite as he took in the sight before him, while Maria's breath hitched at the sight of her estranged husband so vulnerable and yet so despised. She moved closer to Joe, her resolve hardening.

* * * * * * * * * * * * * * * * * *

Chuck Warner's stern visage, once the embodiment of control and manipulation, now contorted in a mix of confusion and fear. His gray hair, disheveled from sleep, seemed less like a crown of power and more like the fur of a cornered animal.

Joe's fingers grazed the cool metal under the pillow—a pistol, oiled and ready. He drew it out and nodded to Maria. She maintained her grip on the rifle, her athletic stance unwavering.

With deliberate slowness, Joe pressed the rifle barrel against Chuck's temple. The subtle nudge was enough to stir the sleeping giant.

Chuck's eyelids fluttered open, his hand instinctively reaching for the weapon now in Joe's possession.

"Looking for this?" Joe's voice was as steady as his aim.

Chuck's sneer twisted into a smirk at the sight of Maria. "Ahhh, my Queen has returned to me."

From the bed's other side, Robbin bolted upright. "What's happening?" Her voice cracked, laden with fear and confusion.

Joe kept his gaze locked on Chuck. "Your

boyfriend has been a bad boy, and it's time to pay the piper."

Robbin clutched the sheet to her chest. "He's no boyfriend of mine." Her voice broke as she recounted the horror of her night with Chuck. With a look of pure disgust, she spat on him.

Maria swiftly guided Robbin to her feet and toward the door where Claire waited, ready to assist.

Joe leaned closer examining Chucks nude body, a grim smile playing on his lips. "Well, I guess it's true what they say about certain men needing to overcompensate."

Chuck glared up at Joe as he continued to rub salt into fresh wounds. "What are we gonna do with you, Chuck? You've been nothing but trouble."

Maria returned just in time to hear Joe lay out Chuck's situation—the absence of his army, his guards dispatched.

Chuck attempted a final plea. "Let me go... I'll leave you alone... You'll never hear from me again. C'mon Joe you can't kill a man, not in cold blood you can't"

But Joe had heard enough empty promises. "My family comes first," he declared before a shot shattered the stillness.

Blood blossomed from Chuck's head like a macabre flower; his body slumped lifelessly against the sheets.

Joe looked down at Chuck with an expression that bore no satisfaction—only resolution. "That was your final miscalculation."

Maria embraced him tightly as tears streaked her cheeks. "It had to be done," she whispered into his shoulder.

"Yes," Joe agreed as he held her close, their hearts beating together in the aftermath of justice served by their own hands.

Maria's arms still wrapped around Joe, her presence a reassuring weight against his back. They moved together toward the daylight that poured in through the open door. Jojo's eyes met his father's as they emerged, searching for confirmation in the silence that followed the gunshot.

"Dad, is it over?"

Joe's nod carried the weight of finality. "Yeah, it's over. He won't bother us anymore."

A collective sigh rippled through them, and like branches intertwining after a storm, they huddled close. Tears fell freely, a mixture of grief and relief painting their cheeks.

Claire's gaze drifted to Robbin, who stood

slightly apart, her body trembling like a leaf in the wind. "You okay?"

Robbin managed a nod. "I guess so... I just can't believe all this."

"Come with us," Claire offered, her voice a lifeline amidst the chaos. "You'll be safe."

Robbin hesitated, lost in thought. "My family... gone. Nothing left for me here in Center Hill." A glimmer of hope sparked in her eyes. "I'd like that— feeling safe again."

Their quiet moment fractured as townspeople converged on the trading post, their whispers building into a cacophony of curiosity and concern.

Joe hoisted himself onto an old car hood, his figure casting a long shadow across the murmuring crowd.

"Chuck Warner brought darkness to your town," Joe began, his voice steady and clear. "He sowed the same seeds in Leesburg before we drove him out. We've been on his trail, and now... he's gone for good."

A wave of cheers washed over them, carrying away some of the heavy air that had settled on their shoulders.

Joe continued, outlining the skeleton of a society reborn from the ashes. "Find trustworthy leaders.

Build a force to keep peace and a court for justice." His words were nails and wood to construct their future. "United you stand strong—protect your town."

The crowd's cheer swelled again; Joe's words had struck a chord.

"Will you lead us?" someone called out.

The question echoed as more voices took up the chant. "Lead us!"

Joe's eyes sought Maria's as he grappled with the weight of their plea. Her nod was subtle but full of trust.

"I'm tired," he admitted to them all. "I want to be with my family." The crowd fell silent, expectant.

A lone voice cut through. "Please help us start... we trust you."

Maria squeezed Joe's hand; her eyes spoke volumes—she believed in him.

Joe faced the crowd once more, determination etched into his features. "Okay," he conceded, his voice ringing with resolve. "I'll stay to help lay your foundation." He jumped down from his makeshift podium to stand among them—ready to lead once more.

* * * * * * * * * * * * * * * * * * *

Joe squinted at the horizon, the sun dipping low, painting the sky in strokes of orange and crimson. Maria's silhouette stood beside him, the dying light catching in her ponytail. He rubbed his beard, a mixture of contemplation and fatigue etched into his features.

"Where do I even begin, this is a monumental task?"

Maria turned to him, her warm brown eyes reflecting the weight of his words. "Joe, begin with exactly what you told them to do. They now have a leader, the next task is to build a police force, find good people that want to protect the town, then find good people to make up a fair court system. Then hold elections for someone to take over so you can get back home." Her lips curled into a knowing smile as she finished with a chuckle. "Easy enough, right?"

"Yeah sure, easy enough." His voice carried a hint of sarcasm as he looked back at the makeshift camp that had become their charge.

Turning away from the sunset, Joe made his way back to where his group had gathered. The murmur of their conversation ceased as they awaited his approach.

He scanned the faces before him—Claire's determined gaze, Miguel's stoic nod, Jake's reassuring smile—and took a deep breath. "I'm staying to help set up some sort of government for these people." His declaration hung in the air like a challenge. "Claire, Miguel, Jake," he continued with a nod toward each one, "I need you three to take Robbin back to the warehouse and keep everything there protected."

Claire straightened her shoulders, ready for action. Miguel crossed his arms but gave an affirming tilt of his head. Jake simply tapped his heart twice in silent agreement.

"Jojo," Joe's gaze shifted to his son who mirrored his father's solid stance, "Sam,"—Sam stood at attention—"and Maria will stay behind and begin the arduous task of getting this town back on its feet again."

A collective breath seemed to be drawn by the group as they processed their new responsibilities.

Joe's eyes softened as he spoke again. "Also," he said with a faint smile that didn't quite reach his eyes, "could you prepare the cabin for me upon my eventual return? I really want some normalcy back in my life."

Murmurs of assent rose from the group. The cabin was more than just walls and a roof; it was hope distilled into wooden beams and nestled among trees.

"Most of the refugees can continue to stay at the warehouse as there is much more room there," Joe added with practicality creeping back into his tone. "They've already started gardens and other preparations."

The group dispersed with purposeful strides. Joe watched them go, each person carrying part of the burden he felt on his shoulders. Maria lingered beside him.

"They'll manage," she assured him softly.

He met her gaze once more before they both set off toward their respective duties — their silhouettes gradually merging with the encroaching night.

The office still smelled of Chuck Warner's cologne, a scent that seemed to linger as stubbornly as the shadow he cast over the town. Joe, Maria, Jojo, and Sam sat around a table scarred with the remnants of hurriedly abandoned business deals. Joe leaned forward, resting his elbows on the surface.

"First things first," Joe began, "Chuck has a huge cache of supplies here that can help these

Once we get some people, we can use some of the weapons and ammo Chuck has stored here to arm them. Come up with some precincts and scheduled shifts for them to patrol. Let's get that done quickly; this town needs protection in a hurry."

Sam straightened in his chair, a determined glint in his eye. "Understood."

Joe's gaze shifted to his son. "Jojo, I need you to find some people willing to sit in judgment of others. They must be trustworthy and respected in the town. You may want to concentrate your efforts on an older demographic, people who aren't as threatening. Ask around town for a few individuals that the townspeople seem to respect and trust and then seek them out and recruit them if you can."

Jojo touched the brim of his beret, a sign of affirmation between soldiers. "Aye-Aye Pops."

Joe sighed heavily, his gaze sweeping over the room as if he could see Chuck lurking in its corners. "I wanna find someplace else for our headquarters as well; I don't like the reminder of Chuck Warner every time I turn around. But we can work on that once we get these supplies distributed. We still need to protect those supplies for now."

The group nodded in agreement, understanding the urgency yet feeling the weight of the tasks ahead.

They rose from their seats and each found a place to bunk down for the night within what had once been Chuck's domain but was now their makeshift command center.

Come morning, they would begin the arduous task of rebuilding this fragile community — piece by piece, person by person — forging something strong from the chaos Chuck Warner had left behind.

CHAPTER THIRTY EIGHT
BUILDING THE FUTURE

Dawn painted the horizon with streaks of pink and orange, its light crawling over the quiet town like a gentle hand rousing sleepers from their dreams. The Kelly family compound, a makeshift fortress in this new world, stirred to life as the first rays kissed the trading post's weathered facade.

Inside, Maria Warner moved with purpose, her athletic frame silhouetted against the rising sun. Her ponytail swayed as she flitted from shelf to shelf, fingers dancing over cans and jars, making mental notes of their supplies. The scent of freshly brewed coffee filled the air, mingling with the morning's crispness.

At a makeshift table, Joe Kelly Jr., known to most as Jojo, sat nursing a steaming cup. He eyed the brew with respect; it was a small luxury in these times. The warmth from the cup seeped into his hands, comforting against the morning chill.

Sam wandered in from outside, his tall frame folding into a chair next to Jojo. "You think there's enough of this black gold to go around?" he asked, accepting a mug from Maria.

She flashed him a smile. "For today, yes. Tomorrow? That's another question."

With mugs in hand and the quiet buzz of conversation building around them, the group shared a moment of calm before branching off to their respective duties.

Sam stood first, stretching his lean figure. "Time to mingle and find our peacekeepers," he said with resolve etched into his features.

Jojo rose as well, placing his beret on his head. "I'll see if there are any level heads for justice," he replied, determination in his voice.

The two men exited into the awakening town as Maria continued her inventory. Each item she checked off brought them one step closer to a semblance of order they were striving to rebuild.

Outside, Sam approached townsfolk with care. He knew trust was hard-earned these days.

"Morning," he greeted a group of men repairing a storefront window. "I'm looking for solid folks willing to wear a badge."

They exchanged glances before one stepped forward. "Might know a guy or two," he said cautiously.

Meanwhile, Jojo found himself at the local diner where townspeople gathered for breakfast and gossip. He slid onto an empty stool at the counter.

"Anyone around here you'd trust with fair judgment?" Jojo asked the server as she poured him more coffee.

She paused, considering his question seriously. "There's Miss Loretta; she used to teach at the high school. Fair but firm," she suggested with a nod.

The morning waned as Sam and Jojo continued their search through the town, weaving between conversations and observations, each interaction bringing them closer to establishing order in their new world while Maria watched over their home base, her mind always calculating what was needed for survival and stability.

* * * * * * * * * * * * * * * * * *

Sam walked briskly through the bustling trading post, scanning the crowd for any sign of the men he had invited earlier that day. He spotted a few familiar faces standing near the makeshift bar, talking quietly amongst themselves.

"Gentlemen," Sam called out as he approached the group. "Glad you could make it. If you'll just follow me, we can meet up with the others."

The men nodded and fell in step behind Sam as he led them towards the back room of the trading post. He had cleared out the storage area earlier, making space for the meeting.

As they entered the room, Sam saw that Joe was already there, along with a handful of men and women. Joe's weathered face broke into a smile when he saw Sam.

"Right on time," Joe said, stepping forward to clasp Sam's hand warmly. "And I see you've brought along some more interested folks. Good, good."

Joe's voice took on a more serious tone as he addressed the full group. "You all know why we're here. This town needs order and justice again. It needs protectors willing to take up that mantle."

Murmurs of assent rippled through the room. Sam felt a swell of pride looking around at those who had answered their call. He knew any one of them would lay down their life for this town.

"Now I don't need to tell you all it's not gonna

be easy," Joe continued, his eyes glinting with determination. "But standing together, we can take back this community. We can show people there's still goodness left in this world."

Another round of agreement followed his words. Sam stepped forward then, ready to outline the plans they had for fortifying the town and establishing a security rotation. As he launched into the details, the sound of footsteps in the hall made him pause.

The door creaked open and Maria slipped quietly into the room, an apologetic look on her face. "Sorry to interrupt," she said. "But everything's squared away in the inventory. I just wanted to let you gentlemen know before I turned in for the night."

Joe gave her a grateful nod. "Thanks Maria. Go get some rest, you've earned it. We'll try not to keep you up with our scheming in here."

Maria smiled, her eyes lingering on Joe for a moment before she slipped back out of the room.

For now, they had work to do. Clearing his throat, Sam continued laying out their plans late into the night, hope for the future burning steadily in his chest.

Sam's voice filled the sparse room, each word underscored by the gravity of their undertaking. "This town is on the brink," he said, locking eyes with each recruit in turn. "It needs us now, not next week, not when it's convenient—tomorrow."

He let the word hang in the air, a call to arms that seemed to settle in the very foundations of the building.

"Tomorrow," he continued, "you'll be sworn in. You'll receive weapons and the authority to enforce this town's laws. You're the line between chaos and order."

The recruits stood in shared silence, understanding the weight of their commitment.

"If there's doubt in any of your hearts, if you've got questions, now's the time to step forward."

The stillness held, unbroken by hesitation or query. A unified resolve knit their faces into a tapestry of determination.

"All agreed then," Sam stated. It wasn't a question but a confirmation of the silent pact they'd all just made.

He scanned their faces one last time before dismissing them with a nod. "Reassemble here at seven in the morning. Get some rest. Tomorrow we start anew."

The recruits dispersed into the night, their footsteps a soft drumbeat against the wooden floorboards, each step an echo of commitment as they left the trading post and vanished into the darkening town.

* * * * * * * * * * * * * * * * * * * *

Sam stood watching them go, his silhouette cut sharply against the dying light. Joe approached from behind.

Sam turned, his face a mask of contemplation etched with lines of responsibility. "We've got twelve men and women," he said, his voice betraying a hint of disappointment. "I'd still like about ten times that number."

Joe stepped beside him, "Don't worry," he replied with a steady voice that carried the weight of experience. "We're here to get them a decent start; they can always recruit more as time goes by."

A nod came from Sam, slow and measured. He pulled off his cap, ran a hand through his short hair, and replaced it with precision. "I know," he conceded, his eyes meeting Joe's with an unspoken understanding between soldiers. "I'm still going back out tomorrow and see what else I can dig up."

Joe's eyes crinkled at the corners as he clapped a firm hand on Sam's shoulder. "That's the spirit," he said, a slight grin breaking through his rugged exterior. "Just remember to keep your head down out there."

Joe looked back up at Sam, squinting slightly. "By the way, have you found a leader among the twelve you've recruited so far? Someone to name as sheriff?"

Sam turned his gaze from the horizon back to Joe. His lips curled into a knowing smile. "I sure have," he said, his chest swelling with pride. "Twenty-two-year career Marine."

Joe's eyebrows shot up. "Awesome. What's his name?"

The grin on Sam's face stretched wider. "Donna."

For a moment, Joe's expression flickered to one of disbelief. "Donna?" he echoed, his voice laced with surprise. "Really? A woman? Are your guys gonna be good with that?"

Sam's chuckle rumbled deep from his chest as he folded his arms across his broad chest. "She won't have any problems, trust me. She commands respect."

Joe absorbed the news, letting it settle in his mind before a slow nod came from him, his earlier astonishment giving way to admiration. "That's awesome, Sam," he said, the edges of his mouth tugging upward in approval. "I think that could be a big factor in the town's trust factor. Way to go, man."

Their shared smile spoke volumes of their mutual respect and the unspoken agreement that strength wasn't gendered—it was earned and Donna had certainly earned it.

Sam turned to Joe, his brow furrowed with concern. "How's Jojo doing with that court he's trying to put together?"

Joe rubbed the stubble on his chin, his gaze drifting toward the wooden building that stood as the town's meeting hall. "I think he's done well," he said, his voice a mix of hope and realism. "He's got six people so far that may or may not be interested."

Sam leaned against the wall, arms crossed. "Sounds tentative."

Joe nodded. "Yeah, most folks are scared as hell to sit in judgment, fearful of reprisals. But we need some law and order around here." He pushed off from the wall, hands sliding into his jeans pockets. "I'm gonna meet with them in the morning. Fingers crossed we can get a court up and running soon."

The silence stretched between them before Sam broke it with a heavy sigh. "Yeah, I'm anxious to get back home too."

Joe glanced over at him, a spark of determination in his eyes. "We will," he assured Sam. "We'll get this place sorted out and then head back."

CHAPTER THIRTY NINE
ESTABLISHING JUSTICE

Sunlight kissed the dilapidated bricks of the old post office as Joe Kelly and his son, Jojo, made their way through the littered streets. Center Hill, once a bustling small town, now held the silence of uncertainty in its air. But today was about change, about stitching the fabric of society back together.

The group stood like relics from a bygone era, their eyes alight with the possibility of purpose. Joe's nod was slow, an unspoken commendation for their punctuality and commitment.

"Good morning," Joe greeted them, his voice carrying the timbre of leadership. "Appreciate y'all being here."

Jojo stepped forward, his posture echoing his father's authority. He introduced himself with a firm handshake that spoke volumes of his military discipline.

As formalities gave way to the heart of the matter, Joe surveyed the faces before him. "Center Hill's got a shot at a fresh start," he began. "But it ain't just gonna happen on its own. Takes good folks like you."

Jojo chimed in, his voice steady, "You're here because your neighbors spoke highly of you. That says something."

Nods and humble smiles met their words as Joe laid out the vision for a resurrected justice system.

"Got ourselves a new sheriff and a team of deputies," Joe continued. "They'll handle the catching, but we need fair-minded folks to handle the judging."

Loretta stepped forward from the group, her resolve as sturdy as her stance. "I'm all in," she declared. "It's time we bring back some order 'round here."

Joe's smile was thin but genuine as he listened to Loretta's suggestion for an odd number of judges. "Loretta, you've got the right idea."

With unanimous raised hands, commitment solidified among them like concrete setting after a storm.

Loretta didn't miss a beat suggesting Richard

Bellamy join their ranks. Agreement rippled through the group with nods and murmurs of support.

"Let's find out if Richard's on board," Joe said, already envisioning this court taking shape. "And remember, justice needs to be blind—no favoritism or personal grudges."

They parted ways with a shared sense of urgency and determination. As Joe and Jojo watched them disperse to seek out Richard Bellamy, there was an unspoken hope that perhaps Center Hill was on its way to becoming a community once again—a place where law and order could flourish amidst chaos.

Joe turned to Jojo, pride shining in his eyes. "That went very well. I think we've got a great start here."

Jojo nodded, arms crossed over his chest. "Yeah, for sure. What else needs to be done, Dad?"

Joe stroked his beard thoughtfully. "Well, we've got a growing police force and a court set up to determine guilt or innocence. The police can use the old station to house any criminals. So we've got security and justice underway."

"That's a hell of a start in just a couple days, Dad," Jojo said, impressed.

"Yeah, indeed." Joe's mouth quirked in a half-smile. "Maria's taken inventory at the trading post. I think we need to get some of those supplies dispersed to the folks who can put them to best use."

Jojo clapped a hand on his father's shoulder. "Let's get back to the trading post and go over that inventory. Figure out where this stuff can be best utilized."

Joe nodded, already picturing the trading post bustling with activity again. "You got it. Let's move."

The two men strode down the street with purpose, invigorated by the progress made. Though the task of rebuilding was monumental, each accomplished goal fueled their momentum. With strong leadership and community cooperation, order and stability were blossoming amidst the rubble.

* * * * * * * * * * * * * * * * * * * *

The heavy door of the trading post swung open with a creak that seemed to echo the weight of the new world they were shouldering. Joe and Jojo stepped into the dim interior, their boots thudding against the worn wooden floor. Maria looked up from her inventory list, strands of hair escaping her ponytail to frame her face.

"How did it go?" she asked, her brown eyes

searching theirs for clues.

Joe dusted off his jeans, his voice steady. "Better than expected. We've got six judges on board. We're aiming for an odd number, so we're bringing in one more — someone we all trust."

Maria nodded, her gaze flickering with approval. "That's progress. And what's next?"

Joe's fingers brushed over a tabletop as he spoke. "Now we take stock of what we've got here. We need to make sure it gets to those who can use it best."

She leaned in, eager to contribute. "We have seeds — lots of them — just sitting in bags. They need to get into the hands of farmers."

"And there's more," Maria continued, ticking off items on her fingers. "Generators, a limited supply of fuel, weapons, ammunition..."

Joe's mind churned like the engine of one of those generators as she listed the resources.

"Let's put up notices for farmers needing seed," he decided with swift resolve.

Maria listened as Joe outlined his plan for the generators and his idea for a food bank.

"Those are great ideas, Joe," she said with a warmth that matched her eyes.

He paused, a furrow forming on his brow. "What

am I missing, Maria? What else needs doing?"

She shook her head, smiling faintly. "You're going above and beyond."

But Joe wasn't satisfied. "I keep thinking about the founding fathers... what they must've envisioned for the future."

"Well," Maria ventured after a moment's thought, "you've got your judicial system set up, but what about making laws? An executive branch?"

Joe exhaled slowly, the air heavy with unspoken responsibility. "Yeah... that's been nagging at me too. Too much power in one place without checks and balances is dangerous."

He rubbed at his beard, speckled with gray and wisdom.

"Good God," he muttered with a half-grin that didn't quite reach his eyes, "I'll never make it back home at this rate."

Maria rested a hand on Joe's arm, her touch radiating reassurance. "We'll make it, babe. It won't be that long."

Joe sighed, the breath seeming to release some of the tension in his shoulders. "I guess we need to find a mayor and a town council and let them organize some elections." He paused, snapping his fingers. "Oh, how could I forget?"

needs to be set up." Joe met her gaze. "Maria, as a former nurse, I'm leaving that up to you."

Maria nodded slowly, determination glinting in her eyes. "I'll handle it," she affirmed. Her mind was already racing ahead, taking stock of who in town had medical training, what supplies they had on hand, and where they could establish some sort of clinic. It wouldn't be easy, but she had confidence that between her experience and Joe's leadership, they could get it done. For now, she gave Joe's arm a grateful squeeze, heartened that even amidst the chaos, he was still looking out for the community's wellbeing.

"Alright, one thing at a time," Joe said, some of the tension leaving his face. He glanced around the trading post, as if seeing it with fresh eyes. "Let's finish up here. We've got people counting on us."

Maria nodded, falling into step beside him as they resumed taking inventory. The weight of rebuilding pressed heavily, but they would carry it together.

CHAPTER FORTY
RETURNING TO HOME

As the weeks turned into a steady march of progress, Joe Kelly watched the cogs of a once-quiet town spring to vibrant life under his guidance. His hands, coarse from days of hard work, rested lightly on a railing as he looked out over Center Hill. The community buzzed with a sense of purpose and determination that had been forged in the fires of calamity and rebuilt through the resolve of its survivors. Each new morning was Joe's canvas, and upon it, he painted a masterpiece of order and stability.

Sam, who had once worked silently in the shadows, now commanded the respect of twenty-three dedicated police officers. Each one had been chosen for both their ability to enforce the newly laid laws and their desire to serve a greater good. Their uniforms may have been mismatched and worn, but their badges shone with the sheen of justice reborn.

The judiciary branch had found its pillars too. Nine judges took their solemn oaths, promising to uphold fairness and due process. Each judge would navigate various trials, while a trio would deliberate upon appeals. For the gravest of affairs — where life hung in the balance — the nine would unite to hear those cases, ensuring no single hand tipped the scales.

Meanwhile, an abandoned house had found a new heartbeat through Maria's ceaseless efforts. What was once an empty shell now echoed with the voices of healers and the solace of sanctuary. With adequate rooms for treatment, the building was no longer just a standing structure but a refuge — a place to mend wounds and nurture hope.

Joe had felt the pulse of the town and sought out potential leaders for its next chapter. Conversations and handshakes had led him to individuals of character; trusted faces now assessed and ready to guide. He had spoken to each potential mayor and council member, their integrity confirmed by the words of their neighbors. Temporary they may be, but in their hands rested the trust of a community ready to shape its own destiny.

Elections had been cast on the horizon, a date

marked on calendars two months hence. The flicker of democracy twinkled once more, promising a voice to every woman and man. Campaigns would be run, debates held, and ballots cast—a return to a semblance of normalcy that many had yearned for since the world went dark.

But as the leaves began to turn with the season, painting the town with shades of russet and gold, Joe felt the call of home stir within him. The whisper of familiar woods and the embrace of private walls beckoned.

Gathering Maria, Jojo, and Sam in the evening's quiet, Joe shared his heart's direction. "We've done more than set foundations here," he said, his voice tinged with a bittersweet note. "We've planted the seeds of a future—a future they can now cultivate themselves."

Maria placed a hand on his arm, her strength as unwavering as her dedication. They had weathered the storm, and together, they had risen above the flood. "Yes, Joe," she agreed, her smile a mirror of his resolve. "We can go home now."

Jojo's nod was solemn, his pride for his father an unspoken anthem in the silence. "Let's pack up at dawn," he said, "and take that road back to where it all begins—with family."

Sam stood, a sentinel of the peace they had fostered. "Tomorrow, we head back. We'll leave this town knowing it stands stronger, hopeful, and free."

And so, as the first light of dawn crept across a sky of soft, robin's egg blue, they packed their simple belongings. They had faced the abyss and conquered it — not with fists or fury, but with compassion and relentless courage.

Joe turned to take one last look, his eyes shimmering with the reflection of all they had accomplished. A nod to Maria, a reassuring glance to Jojo and a firm pat on Sam's back solidified the sentiment in his heart.

"We made it," he said, as hope, like the rising sun, warmed his face, "We're going home."

* * * * * * * * * * * * * * * * * * *

Miguel stood at the edge of the warehouse property, his gaze sweeping across the landscape as the setting sun painted the sky with streaks of orange and red. He caught sight of the group as they emerged from the treeline, their silhouettes becoming clearer with each step they took toward him. As they approached, Miguel's stern expression gave way to a faint smile, one that rarely graced his rugged features.

"About time you all showed up," he called out, his voice a blend of mock irritation and genuine relief.

The tension of their journey melted away in the exchange of embraces. Maria wrapped her arms around Miguel, a gesture that spoke volumes about their shared hardships and victories. Even Sam, whose military composure often held him at a distance, allowed himself a brief moment of camaraderie.

Joe clapped Miguel on the shoulder, his eyes searching for an update. "How's the fort holding up?"

"We've reinforced every inch," Miguel replied, thumbing back toward the warehouse-turned-fortress. "The rhythm here's like clockwork now. Hunting's good, fishing's better."

Jojo lingered at the back of the group, his eyes scanning for a particular figure not present in the welcome party. "And Claire?" he ventured cautiously.

Miguel's eyes narrowed just enough to send an unspoken warning. "She's good," he stated flatly. "Told me about you two."

Silence descended as Joe turned to his son, surprise etching lines deeper into his weathered face. "What? Is that true, Jojo?"

Jojo shuffled his feet, finding sudden interest in the dirt beneath his boots. "Yeah," he admitted softly. "Wasn't planning on broadcasting it just yet."

Joe let out a slow breath, the hint of a smile playing at his lips. "Well then, I'm happy for you both. But you better make sure you treat her well or I have a feeling Miguel here might just rip your head off." He turned back to Miguel with a jesting tone. "Just make sure this one doesn't get out of line."

Jojo offered a nervous chuckle, keenly aware of Miguel's protective nature. "Believe me, that was another reason secrecy seemed like the best way to go."

Miguel stepped forward, his presence formidable yet not unkind. "I'm okay with it," he said to Jojo directly. "You're alright in my book. But your father is right, if you hurt her, I will rip your head off."

Sam couldn't contain himself any longer; laughter erupted from him as he clapped Jojo on the back. "You hear that Bones? Better be on your A-game."

CHAPTER FORTY ONE
UNEXPECTED REVELATIONS

The last leg of their journey left their muscles aching and their hearts heavy with anticipation. When the warehouse came into view, relief washed over the weary travelers like a long-awaited rain. The refugees emerged, faces etched with the stories of their own trials, yet their eyes brightened at the sight of new arrivals. They converged in a tangle of outstretched arms and weathered smiles.

Taylor shifted Parker to her hip, her daughter's curly hair bouncing with each step. Parker clapped her hands, her giggles piercing the solemn air as they were enveloped by loved ones. Jake's arm wrapped protectively around his wife's waist, his other hand tousling Parker's hair. Paulette's face, lined with the marks of a hard-lived life, softened into something resembling peace as she was drawn into hugs that whispered of forgiveness. Toni, small but sturdy, received each embrace with a grace that belied her years.

Jojo scanned the crowd with a soldier's precision, his heart hammering against his ribs. His family's warmth enveloped him in turn, but his eyes kept darting past them until they landed on Claire. Her figure cut through the throng, determination in every stride.

She crashed into Jojo with a force that nearly bowled him over. Arms locked around each other, they stood as a single entity amid the chaos.

"I've missed you so much," he murmured against her ear.

Claire pulled back just enough to look at him, her voice low and steady. "I've missed you too, Jojo. I can't wait any longer... I want to share your bed."

Jojo blinked in surprise. "What happened? I thought we agreed to keep this under wraps?"

Claire held his gaze, fierce and unapologetic. "When you were gone, I thought I'd lost you forever. I made a promise to myself — if you came back... no more secrets." Her lips curved in defiance. "I've been shouting it from the rooftops since I got here."

He let out a breath he hadn't realized he was holding. "It's actually a relief... no more sneaking around." He hesitated before adding, "I thought Abby coming between us in that shed would ruin everything."

"I was hurt," Claire admitted. "But Abby cleared things up for me. Believe it or not, we've grown close."

Jojo's brows knitted together in confusion.

Claire took his hand and started walking towards the warehouse doors. "There's something about Abby... she needs us now — her and Robbin."

Puzzlement clouded Jojo's features as he matched Claire's pace.

"Just wait until we get inside," she said with urgency tinging her voice. "You'll see."

* * * * * * * * * * * * * * * * * * * *

Joe's eyes narrowed as they stepped into the dimly lit warehouse, the smell of oil and old metal hanging heavy in the air. The space was cavernous, a labyrinth of stacked crates and forgotten machinery. Maria followed close behind, her ponytail swaying with each purposeful step.

Claire stood before them, her posture taut with urgency. "A lot has happened while you were away," she announced, her voice a blend of excitement and concern.

Joe's gaze met Claire's, a silent demand for clarity etched into his weathered features. "Claire, what are you talking about?"

Without a word, Claire turned on her heel and strode down the hallway, her boots thudding against the concrete. The group fell in step behind her as she led them to a nondescript door at the end of the corridor. She rapped sharply on the wood, and a muffled voice beckoned from within.

"Come in."

The door swung open to reveal Abby and Robbin propped up in beds, their faces drawn but glowing with an odd serenity. Joe's brow furrowed as he took in the scene.

"What's up? Are you guys sick or something?" Joe's voice echoed with concern as he stepped closer.

Maria's hand flew to her mouth, her eyes widening with dawning comprehension. "Oh my God," she whispered.

Joe looked between Abby and Robbin, confusion turning to alarm. "What's wrong? What's going on?"

Maria's grip tightened on Joe's arm. "Joe," she said forcefully, "They're both pregnant."

"Pregnant?" Joe blinked in surprise. A broad

smile cracked his rugged face. "That's wonderful! Congratulations to you both." He clapped his hands together, his voice booming with cheer. "Who are the fathers? We have to congratulate them as well. I'm so happy for you both. We need to have a celebration."

Maria's hand was a vise on Joe's arm now, her nails digging into his flesh. "JOE!"

He turned to her, irritation flaring at her interruption. "What?"

Her eyes locked onto his, an intensity there that sent a chill down his spine. "Don't you remember what Abby told us? Do you remember where we found Robbin?"

Joe's jubilation drained away as realization dawned on him like cold dawn light filtering through storm clouds.

"Oh my God."

AFTERWORD

I want to thank you once again for taking the time to read this book, and I truly hope I was able to entertain you for a bit.

It is a series, so there is definitely more to come.

I want to take this opportunity to invite you to visit my website and let me know what you think about this book as well as the series. It would mean a great deal to me to be able to interact and get your thoughts for the future of this series. You can not only interact but also join my newsletter to get all the latest on new releases and behind the scenes info on this series and others that will be coming in the near future.

If you're so inclined you can reach that site at:

BrunoBrennan.com

Or you can simply use the QR code below to reach my website

BrunoBrennan.com

Also if you are enjoying the series please leave a review on Amazon. It means so much and lets others know about the series and your thoughts. Just follow the link to review the book on my website

Again, thank you so much for your continued support it really does mean so much to me.

Bruno Brennan

www.ingramcontent.com/pod-product-compliance
Lightning Source LLC
Chambersburg PA
CBHW030631020726
47493CB00006B/1658